"YOU PLANNING A WAR?"

The storekeeper looked up as Flagan Sackett asked for four hundred rounds of .44 caliber ammunition.

"No, sir, I ain't. But if anybody comes a-looking I wouldn't want them to go away disappointed."

"The Dunns have been around! They've been talking against you."

"Talk never scratched any hides," I said. "They've got to do more than talk."

"That's what we came to town for," Curly's voice said from behind me. "I'm going to whip you right down to your socks."

"You'd have trouble," I said, "because I ain't wearing any."

And then he hit me.

Bantam Books by Louis L'Amour
Ask your bookseller for the books you have missed

Sackett Titles by
Louis L'Amour

Louis L'Amour
Galloway

BANTAM BOOKS
TORONTO • NEW YORK • LONDON • SYDNEY • AUCKLAND

GALLOWAY

A Bantam Book / July 1970

2nd printing ... August 1970	*14th printing ... January 1979*
3rd printing . September 1971	*15th printing ... January 1979*
4th printing ... January 1973	*16th printing ... January 1979*
5th printing ..... May 1974	*17th printing ..... May 1979*
6th printing . September 1974	*18th printing ..... June 1980*
7th printing .... March 1975	*19th printing ..... May 1981*
8th printing ..... July 1975	*20th printing ... August 1981*
9th printing .... March 1976	*21st printing ... January 1982*
10th printing ... January 1977	*22nd printing ..... June 1982*
11th printing ... August 1977	*23rd printing ..... April 1983*
12th printing ..... April 1978	*24th printing ..... June 1984*
13th printing ... August 1978	*25th printing ..... June 1985*

26th printing ... March 1986

ISBN 0-553-25510-X

Published simultaneously in the United States and Canada

PRINTED IN THE UNITED STATES OF AMERICA

H   35 34 33 32 31 30 29

Chapter I

The old elk walked up the knoll where the long wind blew. The wolves followed.

The elk realized what was happening, but he didn't know it was only a part of something that had been going on since life began.

He didn't know that it was because of these wolves or their kindred that he had been strong, brave, and free-running all his past years. For it was the wolves who kept the elk herds in shape by weeding out the weak, the old, and the inept.

Now his time had come, and the wolves were there. He no longer had the speed to outrun them nor the get-about to outfight them, and there were four wolves working as a team, not one of them weighing less than a hundred pounds and two of them nearly twice that.

All he had going for him was his wisdom, and so far he was making a fair country try in getting himself to a place where he could make a stand. You could see, plain as the snow on the mountains yonder, that he was heading for the rocks where he could get his back to the wall.

His trouble was that wolves, like Indians, are patient. They had hunted elk before, had seen all of this happen many times, and they knew they were going to get that elk.

They didn't know about me. Coming up as I had, they'd caught no wind of me, nor could they guess it was my work they were doing. For I was figuring on having most of that elk myself.

When a man has been on the run and hasn't had a bite in three days, he's ready to eat an elk—head, hoofs, and horns—all by himself. Trouble was, I'd no way of killing an elk . . . or anything else, really, and if those wolves got the idea I was as bad off as I was they might take right in after me.

A lobo is too smart to harry a man unless he's down and well-nigh helpless. They don't like the man smell, which always means trouble, but a wolf is born with a keen sense of something ready for the kill . . . which I was. Up to a point, I was.

My feet were raw and bloody, the flesh churned into a bloody mess by running over the broken rock, gravel, and stubble of the desert. My body was worn with hunger, thirst, and exhaustion to a point where I could scarcely walk. But there was that inside me, whatever it was that made me a man, that was a whole long way from being whipped.

The wolves could smell blood, they could smell a festering wound, but could they smell the heart of a man? The nerve that was in him?

That elk sprinted for the rocks and the wolves taken in after him, wary of his hoofs, shy of the vicious drive of those forefeet that could stab and cut a wolf to a cripple. The horns didn't worry them too much, but a wolf is a shrewd hunter and wants to lose no hide for his meal.

My instinct is for mountains. The Sacketts of our branch were mountain people, hill folk from Tennessee, and when trouble showed it was our way to take to the hills again. At least until we got our second wind. That was why I pointed toward the mountains yonder.

Ever since I'd got shut of those Jicarilla Apaches I'd

been heading for the hills, but they hadn't left me much to go on. I was making no complaints. If they still had me by this time I'd be dead . . . or wishing I was.

Somebody back yonder stirred up a pack of trouble and those Apache warriors had taken off like somebody'd set their breechclouts afire, leaving me with the squaws.

Now squaws are no bargain. They take to torturing with genuine pleasure. Thing was, when the warriors taken off they also took all the ponies in camp, so I just cut loose and started to run.

The squaws came close to catching me, with my hands tied and all. But I was a long-legged man, barefooted and stark naked and knowing what would happen if they caught me. When the warriors returned they taken after me, too.

By that time I was afar off and had gotten my hands free, and was just beginning to run. All that day and into the night I ran . . . maybe fifty miles . . . but an Apache is like a hound on the trail. So they were back yonder coming after me, and if I didn't get something to eat I was a finished man.

The elk had got the rock behind him and turned to fight, but for the time those wolves were just a-setting there, looking at him, their tongues hanging out.

There was scattered cedar where I lay, and I kept my eyes open for a club, a-wishing all the time for Galloway to show up. But for all I knew he was miles away down in New Mexico.

Worming my way along the ground, I got closer to the wolves. It wasn't going to do me a sight of good to come up on them until they'd made their kill. I was sorry for the elk, but it was no use. If this bunch didn't get him the next would.

Sure enough, when I was still sixty, seventy yards away that elk turned too far after one wolf and another one slipped in behind and hamstrung him. The elk went down, making a game fight of it, but he had no chance.

About that time I got to my knees, yelled, and threw a rock into their midst.

You never seen the like. That rock lit close to one big wolf with a cropped ear and he jumped like he'd been hit. Maybe sand from the ground stung him. Anyway, they turned to stare at me, waving my arms and yelling.

They backed up as I rose to my feet and started slowly toward them. I was holding two stones and I could fling passing well, so I let drive again and had the luck to hit one on the leg.

He jumped and yelped, so I flung the other and they backed up, getting the smell of me now. If those wolves taken a notion I was in as bad shape as I was I'd have had no more chance than the elk, but wolves have always feared man and these were no exception.

Just then I saw a dead cedar, limbs all spread like something had dropped in the middle of them. I picked up a branch longer than my arm and about as thick as my wrist and started on.

The wolves taken off.

They ran off a ways and I limped up to the elk. It was dead.

The wolves stopped a hundred yards or so off and sat down to watch. They hadn't given up by a long shot, but there was a whole lot about me that troubled them.

Naked as I was, I must have looked uncommonly white to them, and that was all wrong according to their notion of men. And they could smell the blood from my feet and maybe the festering that was there. One of the wolves had gone over where I'd been lying and was smelling around to see what his hillside newspaper would tell him. I could guess he was reading a lot out there that I wished he didn't know.

Yet I had a good club in my hands, my back to a cliff, and meat enough to feed me into health again if I could get it cut up. I also needed that hide.

The rock against which the elk had chosen to make

his stand was about thirty feet high and sloped off another twelve feet or so that was mostly broken rock. Some of it was obsidian.

I found myself a good chunk of the right length and began chipping away at it with another rock. I'd seen Indians make arrowheads and when a boy back in the mountains had sometimes made small hunting arrows for my own bow. The Cherokees we grew up around showed us how.

What I wanted now was a knife, and I began chipping away. Those wolves weren't about to leave that much meat, but my chipping made them wary, as wild animals are of anything strange.

After I'd worked awhile on the knife I picked up some dried wood and put it together where it would be handy. My knife was still not in the shape I wanted, but it had a cutting edge and with it I started skinning the elk. When I had peeled back enough of the hide I cut two pieces off and tied them around my feet with strips of the same hide. Even looking at the condition of my feet made my stomach turn over with fear, for they were bloody, torn, and shapeless. But the covering of wet hide made it easier to stand on them and using my club for a cane, I began to hobble around.

The cliff where the elk had made his stand was a thirty foot drop-off at the end of a long, steep mountainside, and among the rocks at its base was all the junk that had fallen down the mountain. Plenty of dried wood, and a wide variety of rocks. What I hunted was iron pyrites, and I found several chunks and broke off two pieces to use in starting a fire.

Beside the elk I made a small pile of shredded bark, crumbled dry leaves and slivers, and then I tried striking the two chunks of iron pyrites together. The sparks came easy, but it taken nearly an hour to get one into the shredded leaves and bark. Then I coaxed it, blowing gently to get a flame going.

Once a tiny flame began I fed it carefully with more bark and then with some slivers of pitch pine until it was blazing nicely. When those flames leaped up and began to crackle I felt like morning on the first day. It was no time at all until I had a steak broiling on a stick propped over the fire. Then I went back to work on my knife.

The wolves showed no mind to leave, and I didn't blame them, so I cut out a few chunks of meat I wasn't going to want and threw them out. They sniffed kind of cautious, then gobbled them up, but they looked surprised, too. Nobody had ever fed them before, seemed like.

In the back of my thoughts there was knowledge of those Jicarillas. They'd be of no mind to give up, and my bloody feet had blazed a pretty easy trail for them.

Keeping my fire alive I skinned out the rest of that elk, scraped some fat off the hide, and cut out the best chunks of meat. I broke off a couple of pieces of antler because it makes a good tool for chipping stone, then I bundled those cuts of meat into the elk hide, whilst ever and anon I tossed a bone or something to those wolves whose kill I had taken.

I understood how they felt, for they had been hungry, too.

My eyes kept straying to the country south of me, but I could see no movement, nothing. With Apaches your first look is often your last one.

Putting out my fire, dropping the two pieces of iron pyrites into the hide along with the meat, I swung the hide over my shoulder and taking up my staff, I moved out. Following the face of the cliff, I started north. Behind me the wolves were snarling and tearing at the carcass.

"Flagan Sackett," I said to myself, "you owe those wolves. You surely do."

It was slow going. The meat and hide were a burden, and in spite of the elk skin on my feet it was all I could do to step on them. What I needed was a hideout, a place where I could rest up and let my feet heal . . . if they would.

The desert had run out behind me. Low green hills broken by jagged outcroppings and covered by clusters of aspens or scattered pines lay before and around me. Twice I followed the crests of ridges, hidden by the scattered trees, scouting the land as I went.

It was a wild, lonely country with occasional streamers of snow in the shadows where the sun did not reach. The wind was cold off the mountains and I was a naked man with enemies behind me and nothing before me but hope.

Once I lowered my pack to gather some snakeweed that I found in a hollow, and blessed my mountain boyhood where a body had to scrape and scrabble to live.

When I could go no further I worked my way back into a willow clump where rising smoke would be scattered by the leaves and branches. Then I built a small fire of dry wood that gave almost no smoke, and made a vessel from bark. Dipping up some water from the creek I put it to boil on a stick suspended above the fire, and put some snakeweed into it. When the snakeweed had boiled for a time I bathed my feet with it, using a few handfuls of soft sage for a cloth. Meanwhile I broiled more meat.

The day had ruined my crude moccasins so I staked out the hide, scraped it some more, and cut out another pair made a little better.

After I'd eaten, during which time I moved my fire a few feet, I worked at my knife of obsidian, chipping away to get a good edge. I was clumsy. I'd seen Indians do it in a third of the time. Then I moved my fire again, scattered pine needles over the warm ground where the fire had been, and curled up there with the elk hide over me.

Just a-wishing wouldn't take me there, but my thoughts kept drifting back to the mountain cabin where I was born, back nigh to Denney's Gap, in Tennessee. That old cabin had been mighty comfortable, poor as it was, but unless some squatter had moved into it the cabin was alone now, and empty.

In the cold of dawn the birds were telling stories in the brush, and that spoke well of the neighborhood. As happy as they sounded it was unlikely there was anything hateful around.

My feet were sore and the muscles of my calves ached from the awkward way I'd walked trying to spare my feet. I got up, but my first step hurt so that tears came to my eyes. I sat back down, scared to think of the trouble I was in.

This was no place to stop. I had to start on again, no matter what. Suddenly the eye caught movement on the slope, and when I turned my head I saw the wolf.

It was the one with the cropped ear, and he was watching me.

Chapter II

What had become of the others I did not know, but this one was there, and I remembered it well.

"Howdy, boy!" I said, and taking up a scrap from near the fire, I threw it out toward him.

He stood up then, started forward, then stopped. Turning my back on him I shouldered my pack, and taking my club in my hand, I started along the mountain.

When I came out into the open I looked back down the mountain. Far below and far away I could see something moving . . . several men.

My throat kind of tightened up on me. They were still coming then, and that meant I hadn't a chance in the world. Not one.

If they stayed on my trail they were sure to get me.

The wolf had come up to where I had thrown the scrap of meat and was sniffing it.

My trouble started when Galloway and me decided to go to ranching. We wanted to find ourselves some fresh country not all cluttered up with folks. We wanted to settle somewhere in the mountains or with mountains close by, and we wanted land where there was grass and water.

We had us a talk with Tell Sackett and old Cap

Rountree, and both of them told us about the country around the Animas, Florida, and La Plata rivers. It seemed that it would be a good idea to take a ride out thataway and sort of prospect the country.

Galloway had been helping Parmalee Sackett with a herd of cattle he'd bought in Arizona awhile back, so I decided to go ahead and scout the country my own-self. It was as fine a ride as ever I had until I come up on those Apaches.

They spotted me and they came in after me and I decided to show them some distance, so I swung my horse around and taken out of there. About the fourth jump my horse took, his hoof went into a gopher hole and he spilled us both. I came up with my eyes and ears full of sand, my rifle on the underside of the horse, which had a broken leg, and those Indians came sweeping down on me.

There were too many of them to fight so I decided to try to face them. Indians are notional, and it just might be that no shooting and a brave face might change their way to favor me.

So I just walked out to meet them, and when they showed up I cussed them out in Apache, as much of it as I knew, and told them that was no way to treat a friend.

Well, it didn't work. They bound my hands and feet and taken me back to camp. They were all set to find out how tough a man I was, and they began it by stripping my clothes off and staking me out in the sun. They hung a water bag close to my head with water dripping from it drop by drop within inches of my mouth, but they'd give me none of it.

The youngsters around camp and some of the squaws would come around and throw sand in my face or beat me with sticks, sometimes for a half hour at a time. All they got out of me was a lot of cussin', so they decided to try something really good.

Whilst they were setting around the fire talking it over, I did some business on my own account.

One of the youngsters had dropped his stick when he got tired of beating me and it lay across my chest. By humping myself up I slid it down toward my mouth, got it into my teeth and tilted it up until the drops from that waterbag were coming down it toward my mouth.

At first most of the drops fell off onto the ground, but I hung onto that stick like a bulldog and sure enough after awhile some drops began to get into my mouth. Not that it was much, but when a body has been so long without water the slightest drop feels mighty, mighty good.

My jaws began to ache and my neck got stiff but I daren't move for fear I'd lose the stick or the water would start dribbling another way.

All of a sudden one of the Indians noticed what I was doing and called the others. Well, sir, you never heard such laughing and chuckling. They all gathered around, pointing and talking. It was a new thing, what I'd done, and they admired me for being game, but that didn't change them none. After they had all seen it one of the braves reached over and jerked that stick from my jaws so hard he nigh taken some teeth with it. I cussed him for a no-account coyote and a dog-robber, and he kicked me.

All night I lay there, staked out on the sand with no water and less hope. Once a tarantula crawled across my belly, going about his own affairs, and the ants found some of the cuts left from the stick beatings. Come daylight they untied my feet and led me to an anthill where they had stakes driven into the ground, and I could see what they were planning.

Of a sudden there was a shot, then a yell, some moaning cries, and every Apache in the lot jumped his pony and rushed off after whatever it was.

And when they lit out, I did likewise.

We Sackett boys run to length, and I was always a fair to middlin' foot racer, so I taken off like a scared jackrabbit, paying no mind to the broken rock and

gravel underfoot. And those squaws came after me, a-
yellin' their lungs out.

Now the men were closing in on me, and with my
feet in the shape they were in I surely wasn't going far,
nor could I hope to outrun them. The only thing in
my favor was that we were heading right into Ute country. Not that I'd be any better off in the hands of Utes,
but the Apaches didn't find any welcome in Ute country,
either. The further they got into Ute country the more
worried those Apaches were going to be.

Walking on pine needles was a lot better than rock
and the like, but what I needed was a hiding place,
and after that I needed some kind of weapon.

Deliberately I chose the steeper, less likely ways.
Climbing steps were no more painful than those on the
level, yet they would take me to places the Indians
could not follow on their ponies.

Pulling myself up through a narrow space between
two boulders I edged along a rim of rock and then
climbed a dry waterfall to the level above. My feet
were bleeding again, but I found some red clay that
I could mix with pinon gum and tallow from the elk
fat to make a salve often used by the Navajo to pro-
mote healing. Yet when I looked back and down I
could see eight Apaches, close enough to see the color
of their horses.

The Apache fights on his feet, and climbing that
mountain after me would be no trick. They hadn't seen
me yet but when they did, they'd come. Maybe I was a
damned fool, my feet hurting the way they were. Maybe I should just quit and let them kill me. But there
was no give-up in me. We boys in the backwoods
weren't raised thataway. By the time I was fourteen I
knew how to shoot, trap and skin, how to rustle my
grub in the woods, and if need be to get along on less
than a jackrabbit.

Mostly the boys I ran the hills with were Cherokee,
and I learned as much from their folks as my own.

We had only two books in our family, so Ma taught us to read from the *Bible* and *Pilgrim's Progress*.

One thing we learned. To make a start and keep plugging. When I had fights at school, the little while I went, I just bowed my neck and kept swinging until something hit the dirt. Sometimes it was me, but I always got up.

Right now I made a decision. Those Apaches weren't going to take kindly to leaving their ponies behind them in Ute country, so if they killed me they were going to have to do it on top of the mountain. That was where I headed.

Turning crossways of the trail I started climbing, using my hands as much as my feet. Stopping near a clump of aspen I looked back down. Far below I could see them and they could see me, and they were drawn up, staring at me.

There was no sense to shooting. Up hill thataway a body ain't going to hit much and I was a far piece off from them. I could almost hear them talking it over.

My hope was they'd decide I wasn't worth the trouble. But it was a slim hope, so I continued on up the mountain. It was a heartbreaker, almost straight up in places, although there were plenty of hand and foot holds. Then I crawled up on the ledge where lay a dead coyote, and I knew that Apaches wouldn't touch one. Taking it by the tail I gave it a good swing and let it fall toward the trail below, right across the path they would have to follow.

I doubted if it would more than make them uneasy, but it did give me an idea. To an Apache the hoot of an owl is a sign of death, and since boyhood I'd been able to hoot well enough to get answers from owls. Knowing sound would carry in those high canyons, I tried it.

They could no longer see me but I could see them, and at the first hoot they pulled up short, and when they reached the dead coyote they stopped again. So I started a couple of boulders rolling down the mountain. I wasn't likely to hit one of them, but it might worry them a little.

Of a sudden I came into a kind of scooped-out hollow in the side of the mountain. Some of it was meadow, but at the back leading up into the notch that led toward the crest it was mostly filled with aspen. And I knew that was it.

I just wasn't going any further.

Crawling back into those aspens where they grew tight and close together I covered my way as well as possible and just lay down. My feet felt like fire, and my legs hurt all the way up. Below the knees, from favoring the soles, the muscles were giving me hell. I just stretched out under the leaves and lay there.

They could find me, all right; but they'd have to hunt.

My club clutched in my hand, I waited, listened for the slightest sound. The aspens whispered and somewhere a bird or small animal rustled in the leaves, but they did not come. Finally I just fell asleep. I had no idea how or when . . . I just did.

Hours later the cold awakened me. All was still. I lay there for awhile, then slowly sat up. It brought kind of a groan from me, which I swallowed before it got too loud. I couldn't see anything or hear anything, so I just naturally lay back down, dug deeper into the leaves, and went to sleep again.

When next I awakened it was morning, and I was stiff with cold. Crawling out of the aspens I looked around, but saw nothing of the Apaches.

Gathering up my pack I limped out through the groves of aspen and began to work my way down into an interior canyon. After an hour, in a hollow under some trees and boulders I stopped, built a small fire of dry, smokeless wood and broiled an elk steak. Hearing a faint rustling among the trees I dropped a couple of bones near the remains of my fire, then went on down.

Later in the day I again bathed my feet in a concoction of snakeweed. Whether it was actually helping I did not know, but it felt good and eased the hurt.

For an hour I rested, then started down the stream. Later I found some bee weed, sometimes called stink-weed. The Navajo used it to start fires by friction as the brittle stalks, whirled between the palms, will start a fire in two minutes or less, especially if a little sand is added to increase the friction.

All the time I kept watch on the slope down which I'd come, but I saw nothing of the Apaches. Maybe the owl-hoot death signal had scared them off, or maybe it was the owl-hoot and the dead coyote together or the feeling they were getting into Ute country. Anyway, there was no sign of them.

Not that I was alone. There was something out there in the brush that was a-watching me, and it might be that wolf. A wolf has been known to stalk a man or an animal for miles, and this wolf needed nobody to tell him that I was in a bad way. He could smell the blood and the festering of some of the cuts on my feet. While I was wary of him and trusted him none at all, I still had no blame for him. He was a wild thing that had to rustle its grub as best it could, and I felt sympathy for it, which was the reason I tossed out those fragments of meat or bone.

Yet that night was the worst. The cold was cruel and my naked body could take no warmth from the remains of the elk hide. All night long I shivered, teeth chattering beside the fire that ate fuel like a famished beast so that I almost never ceased from the hunting of it.

Wild and weird were the snow-covered peaks around me, dark the gorge where I shuddered over my fire, the cold seeping through my bones, stiffening my muscles. A wind, cold and raw, came down the canyon, blowing my fire and robbing my body of the little warmth it had.

The night seemed to stretch on forever. Once I slept, awakening to find the wind gone but my fire down to a few tiny coals, and with effort I nursed it back into flame. Something padded in the brush out there so I built my fire higher and kept my club and my stone knife closer.

How many men had crouched beside such fires in the years gone by? With no more weapons than I had?

At last the dawn came, cold and bleak, and I could see where wood lay without blundering through the brush. I built up my fire, then took the hide and cut a piece big enough for fresh moccasins. I buried the piece in the ground nearby to make it soft and pliable for the work to come.

I found some chickweed tubers and ate them and ate the last of the elk meat, throwing the few bones into the brush.

Hobbling up on the slope, I looked the country over with care. Now in most places a man can live if he knows something of plants and animals, and if he will take time enough to think things out. It is a man's brain that has removed him from the animals, and it is man's brain that will let him survive, if he takes time to think.

First, I needed a weapon. Second, I must have shelter and clothing. So I stood there, studying the land to see what it offered.

The canyon had high, rocky sides with forest climbing to the crest. There was a stream in the bottom of the gorge with willows around it, and a good bit of grass and some brush. On the ground not twenty feet away lay a well-seasoned branch fallen from a tree. By breaking off the small branches I could fix an obsidian point on it and have a lance.

The bushy-looking trees with scaly twigs and leaves, kind of silvery in the sunlight, were buffalo-berry. The Indians used to collect them to flavor buffalo or antelope meat. There were some wild roses there, too, and I could see the red of some rose hips. There was plenty of deer sign along the stream, and I might have time to make a bow and some arrows.

Limping down to the buffalo-berry bushes I started eating them, pits and all. I topped them off with some rose hips. They weren't any banquet but they would keep me alive. If no Indians found me.

This was Ute country, but both the Navajo and the Apache came here also.

And, of course, there was the wolf.

Chapter III

There was a pole corral and two lights shining from square windows in the long, low log building. Galloway Sackett swung from the saddle and stood looking into the window for a full minute before he tied his horse.

It was little enough he could see. The window was fly-specked and dirty, but there was a bar inside, and several men. A half dozen horses stood at the hitching rail.

Four of the horses wore a brand strange to him, a Clover Three . . . three figure 3's arranged like a three-leaf clover.

Galloway whipped the dust from his clothes with his hat, then started for the door. A glance at a powerful black horse stopped him. He looked at the brand and whistled softly.

Originally the brand must have been a Clover Three, but now it was a Flower. A reverse 3 had been faced to each of the other 3's, then another set had been added, a stem and tendrils to join the petals to the stem. The job was beautifully done, obviously by a rewrite man who knew his business and enjoyed it.

"That's a man I've got to see," Galloway muttered. "He'd wear a Sherman button to a Georgia picnic!"

He pushed open the door and stepped in, then walked

to the bar. As he crossed the floor he saw four men sitting at a table together, obviously the Clover Three men. In a corner not far from the bar sat another man, alone.

He wore a fringed buckskin hunting shirt, under it a blue shirt, obviously either new or fresh. He wore a low-crowned black hat, and was smooth-shaved except for a reddish mustache, neatly trimmed and waxed.

The man in the buckskin shirt wore two pistols, one butt forward, one butt to the rear . . . a tricky thing, for a man might draw with either hand or both guns at once. On the table were a bottle of wine, a glass, and a pack of cards.

Aside from the scruffy-looking man behind the bar there were two others in the room, a man in a dirty white shirt with sleeve garters, and a hairy old man in soiled buckskins.

Galloway Sackett, who had as much appreciation for situations as the next man, ordered rye and edged around the corner of the bar so he could watch what was happening . . . if anything.

The four riders from the Clover Three looked embarrassed, while the lone man in the buckskin shirt drank his wine calmly, shuffled the cards and laid them out for solitaire, seemingly unconcerned.

Finally one of the Clover Three riders cleared his throat. "Quite a brand you got there, Mister."

Without lifting his eyes from the cards, the other man replied: "You are speaking to me, I presume? Yes, I rather fancy that brand." He glanced up, smiling pleasantly. "Covers yours like a blanket, doesn't it?"

Galloway was astonished, but the four riders only fidgeted, and then the same man said, "The boss wants to talk to you."

"Does he now? Well, you tell him to ride right on in . . . if he has any horses left."

"I mean . . . he's got a proposition for you. After all, it wasn't him—"

"Of course it wasn't. How could he be expected to account for all the stock on his ranches? You tell your boss to come right on into town. Tell him that I'll be waiting for him. Tell him I've been looking forward to our meeting. Tell him I've been wanting to say hello and good-bye."

"Look, Shadow," the Clover Three man protested, "the boss just doesn't have the time—"

"That's right, Will. Your boss doesn't have the time. In fact he is completely out of time." The man called Shadow placed a card, then glanced up. "You tell Pasten for me that if he will turn his remuda loose, fire his hands and ride off the range with what he can carry on his saddle he can go.

"Otherwise," Shadow added, "I will kill him."

Nobody said anything. Galloway Sackett tasted his rye and waited, as they all waited.

Then Will said, "Aw, give him a chance! You know he can't do that!"

"Pasten robbed a lot of people to build his herd. Some of the cattle were my cattle, some of the cattle had belonged to friends of mine. Some of those people are no longer alive to collect what he owes them, but I intend to see that he does not profit from it. You tell him he's got twenty-four hours . . . no longer."

"Look here." One of the punchers started to rise. "You can't get away with that! You—!"

"Twenty-four hours, gentlemen. You ride out and tell him that. I am through talking." His head turned ever so slightly. "As for you, I would suggest you either sit down or draw a gun. The choice is yours."

He spoke mildly, as one might in a polite conversation, and without stress.

Slowly, carefully, the puncher sat down.

Galloway Sackett tasted his rye again and when the bartender came near he said, "I'm hunting a man who knows the San Juan country."

The bartender shrugged, then indicated Shadow with a gesture of his head. "He knows it, but I wouldn't start any talk about it now. He's got things on his mind."

"I also want a horse—a good horse and a couple of pack horses or mules."

"Talk to him." Then the bartender added, "That's a good country to stay out of. There's talk of trouble with the Utes, and the Jicarillas been cutting loose up thataway."

The four men at the table got up quietly and went out of the door, walking carefully. Galloway Sackett finished his drink, then walked over to the other man's table.

"Mr. Shadow? I'm Galloway Sackett."

"It is a name not unknown to me. Sit down, will you? What will you have?"

"I'm going to have some coffee and some grub, but what I really want is information. The bartender told me you knew the San Juan country."

"I do."

"About a week ago I run into a bunch of Jicarillas and they had my brother. They'd started to work on him. I was alone, but figured if I could create a fuss he'd cut loose on his own. I did, and he did."

"He got away?"

"He surely did. And dropped clean off the world. I hunted for him and they did. Those Jicarillas weren't about to lose him so they taken in after him. He was stark naked and had his hands tied, but he got away."

"He's dead, then."

"Not Flagan. We Sacketts don't die easy, and Flagan is a tough man. He's been up the creek and over the mountain. He's fit Comanches and Arapahoes on the buffalo plains, and about ever' kind of man or animal. He's a tough man."

"That San Juan country is tough. It's the most beautiful country in the world, but about two-thirds of it stands on end."

Shadow paused, waiting while the bartender placed

coffee and food on the table. Then he asked, "What do you want me to do?"

"Tell me about it. How the streams run, the best ways to get through the mountains, where I'm liable to run into Indians. I'm going in after him."

"You're bucking a stacked deck, my friend. You'll need an outfit."

"That's another thing. The bartender said you had horses. I need a spare for Flagan to ride when I find him, and I'll need a couple of pack horses for grub and the like."

Shadow took a thin cigar from his pocket and lighted it. He studied the end of it for a moment, then said, "If I didn't have some business to attend to, I'd go with you."

"Twenty-four hours, you gave him. Do you think he'll move?"

"Yes."

Galloway glanced at Shadow thoughtfully. "He must know you, this Pasten gent."

"He knows me. He stole cattle and killed men in the Mimbres country. He wiped out a lot of us, then pulled out and drove the cattle clear out of the country. I took in after him."

"I lost the trail, then found it again. Meanwhile he'd settled down here, hired a bunch of reasonably honest hands, and then he cooked up that Clover Three brand. Guess he had an idea it couldn't be blotted, so I did it, just as a challenge. So he sent a hired man after me, but I remembered the man from Texas, and he did not remember me."

"How'd that happen?"

Shadow shrugged. "I was a teacher at Waco University. Our paths did not cross in a way he would notice."

"You were a teacher?"

He shrugged. "One does what one can. I needed the job, they needed the teacher. In fact, they wanted

me to stay on, but the pay was small and I was restless.
I had come to America to hunt for gold."

He glanced at Galloway again. "Are you related to
Orrin Sackett?"

"He's kin."

"He defended me in a shooting case. My first one,
in fact. It was a little matter of a horse. My horse
was stolen. I hunted the man down and he drew a
pistol and I shot him. Someone advised me to hire
Orrin Sackett and I did . . . fortunately."

They finished their coffee, talked idly of various
things, and then Shadow stood up. "I have a cabin
down the road apiece. If you'd like you may join me.
There's an empty bunk, and you're welcome."

The cabin was small but comfortable. There were
Navajo rugs on the floors, curtains at the windows,
and a couple of dozen books.

"I envy you the books," Galloway said. "School was
a rare time thing for us. Mostly it was Ma teaching us
from the Bible, and she read a couple of stories to
us written by Walter Scott. Flagan an' me, we got our
learning in the woods with our Winchesters."

"Your brother is a woodsman? Not just a cowhand?"

"We grew up in the Cumberland country. We learned
from the Cherokees. Given a chance Flagan could get
along most anywhere."

"Then he might make it. He might just be alive."

It was the first time he had slept in a bed in weeks,
but Galloway slept well, and awakened with the sun.
Shadow was already outside but a minute or two later
he came in.

"I just had word. Pasten left the country. I've started
some men rounding up my cattle, and the others."

Galloway Sackett dressed. Somewhere in the country
far to the north and east his brother was either dead
or fighting for his very existence. Somehow he must
find him. The night before, Shadow had carefully out-
lined the lay of the country, how the rivers ran, the
Animas, the Florida, and the La Plata, and Galloway,

knowing his brother's mind as he knew his own, was trying to figure out what Flagan would have done when he got away.

He would have headed for the mountains, and the first trail he'd found had pointed north. It was Flagan's trail, but that of the Apaches following him as well.

Flagan would head into the hills, try and find some place to hole up. He would need some clothes, and he would need shelter and food. In the mountains, with luck, he could find what he needed.

"Sackett?" Shadow called from the door. "Get your gear together. I've saddled our horses and we're packed for the trip."

"We?"

"I'm going with you."

Chapter IV

For a week I rested beside the creek, keeping hidden when possible. I treated my feet alternately with the salve I had made and leaves of the Datura, and the soles began to heal.

Twice I snared rabbits, once I knocked down a sage hen. There were yampa roots, Indian potatoes, and I found a rat's nest containing nearly a bushel of hazelnuts. The fare was scant but I was making out.

By the end of the week I'd completed a bow and some arrows, and had killed a deer. With the piece of elk hide, softened by its burial in the earth, I made moccasins. Marking out the soles by tracing my feet with charcoal, I then cut out an oval as long as my two feet, cut it in half, and in the middle of each squared-off end I cut a slit long enough for my foot to get into, then cut another slit to make a T. I now had the upper for each moccasin and using a thorn for an awl I punched holes to sew the uppers to the soles. Finally I punched holes along each side of the slit to take a drawstring.

One of the first things I'd done was to make a shelter hidden well back in a clump of willows. Crawling back into the middle of the thickest clump I could find, I cut off some brush, enough to make a sleeping space.

Then I drew the willows together overhead and tied them, allowing others to stand up to mask what I had done.

This wasn't a shelter I built all at once. First I had just crawled among the willows to sleep where I'd not be easily found, then I widened it for more room, and the willows I cut I wove in overhead and around the sides to make it snugger and warmer. After a week of work the tunnel was six feet long and masked by tying two growing willows a little closer together once I was inside.

Twice I saw deer just too far off to risk a shot. The one buckskin I had was not enough to make a shirt.

Living in such a way leaves no time for rest. Between the two slopes, the stream, and the narrow bottom of the canyon, I made out. Several times I caught fish, never large enough, and found clumps of sego lily and ate the bulbs. Gradually over that week the stiffness and soreness began to leave my muscles and my feet began to heal.

Yet I was facing the same thing that faced every hunting and food-gathering people. Soon a man has eaten all that's available close by and the game grows wary. Until men learned to plant crops and herd animals for food they had of necessity to move on ... and on.

Most of what I'd done to make myself comfortable must be left behind, and it worried me that I had no better weapons. My feet were better, but the skin was tender and I daren't walk very far at any one time. I'd been sparing of the hazelnuts for they were the best of my food, but at last they gave out, too. On the ninth day I gathered my few possessions and started out.

Back up at the forks of the creek in Tennessee they don't raise many foolish children, and the foolish ones don't live long enough to get knee-high to a short sheep. This was Indian country, so I taken it easy. My weapons weren't fit for fighting and my feet were too sore for running.

When I'd traveled about a half mile I sat down to study out the land. The canyon was widening out, and there was plenty of deer sign. Twice I saw tracks of a mountain lion, a big one.

By nightfall I'd covered four miles, resting often. The canyon had widened to a valley and the stream joined a larger river that flowed south. I could see the place where they flowed together, right up ahead. North of me the country seemed to flatten out, with towering snow-covered peaks just beyond. Those peaks must be the San Juans Tell Sackett had spoken of. I knew this country only by hear-tell, and when I'd been running ahead of those Jicarillas I'd not been paying much mind to landmarks.

Working my way over to the brush and trees that followed the canyon wall, I hunkered down to study out the land. And that was how I saw those Utes before they saw me.

They were coming up from the south and they had about twenty riderless horses with them, and a few of those horses looked almighty familiar. They passed nigh me, close enough to see they were a war party returning from some raid. They had bloody scalps, and it looked like they had run into those Jicarillas. Ambushing an Apache isn't an easy thing to do but it surely looked like they'd done it.

Trying to steal a horse ran through my mind, but I made myself forget it. My feet were in no shape for travel and I couldn't stand another chase. My best bet was to head east toward the Animas where I'd heard there were some prospectors.

Fact is, I was hungry most of the time. What I'd been finding was scarcely enough to keep soul and body together, and down on the flat it was harder to find what I needed. I found some Jimson weed and cut a few leaves to put in my moccasins. I'd used it for saddle sores and knew it eased the pain and seemed to help them to heal, but it was dangerous stuff to fool around with, and many Indians won't touch it.

Studying out the ground I saw a field of blue flowers, a kind of phlox the Navajo used to make a tea that helped them sing loudly at the Squaw Dance, and was also a "medicine" used for the Navajo Wind Chant. But I found nothing to eat until night when I caught a fine big trout in an angle of the stream, spearing it with more luck than skill, and then as I was making camp I found some Indian potatoes. So I ate well, considering.

When the fish was eaten I huddled by my capful of fire and wished for a cabin, a girl, and a meal waiting, for I was a lonesome man with little enough before me and nothing behind but troubles. Soon a cricket began to sing near my fire, so I made care to leave him be. There's a saying in the mountains that if you harm a cricket his friends will come and eat your socks. A hard time they would have with me, not having socks or anything else.

Galloway was no doubt eating his belly full in some fine restaurant or house, filling up on beef and frijoles whilst I starved in the woods. It is rare enough that I feel sorry for myself but that night I did, but what is the old saying the Irish have? *The beginning of a ship is a board; of a kiln, a stone; and the beginning of health is sleep.*

I slept.

Cold it was, and the dew heavy upon the grass and upon me as well, but I slept and the wind whispered in the aspen leaves, and in the darkness the taste of smoke came to my tongue, and the smell of it to my nose. Cold and dark it was when the smell of it awakened me, and I sat up, shivering with a chill that chattered my teeth. Listening into the night I heard nothing, but then my eye caught a faint gleam and I looked again and it was a dying fire, not fifty yards off.

Slowly and carefully I got to my feet. Indians. At least a dozen, and one of them awake and on guard. They must have made camp after I fell asleep, although it was late for Indians to be about, but come daylight they would surely find me. Easing my feet into my moccasins, I gathered what I had to carry and slipped away. When I was well away from their camp and in the bottom, I started to run.

The earth was soft underfoot, and the one thing I needed now was distance. They would find my camp in the morning and come after me. I ran and walked for what must have been a couple of hours, and then I went into the stream.

The moon was up and the whole country was bathed in such a white beauty a man could not believe, the aspens silvery bright, the pines dark and still. The cold water felt good to my feet but because the current was swift and the footing uncertain, I took my time. After awhile I came out on the bank and sat down, my muscles aching and weary, my feet sore. Carefully I dried them with handfuls of grass and clumps of soft sage.

Light was breaking when I started again. Within the hour they would be on my trail, and they would move much faster than I could. I did not know the Utes, but the stories I'd heard were mixed, and this was their country.

Now I moved from rock to rock, carrying a small flat rock in my hand to put down wherever I might leave a footprint. The rock left a mark but it was indefinite and might have been caused by any number of things. The Utes might find me, but I did not intend it should be easy, and I could drop the rock I carried and step from it to some other surface that would leave no mark.

Something rustled in the brush. Turning sharply I was only in time to see leaves moving where something had passed by. Crouching near a rock, I waited, but nothing came. Moving toward the brush, spear poised, I found only the faintest of tracks . . . the wolf.

He was with me still, a rare thing for a lone wolf to stalk a man for so long a time. Yet he was out there now, in the brush, stalking me for a kill. Still, there must be easier game.

Twice I made my way through thick groves of aspen, trying to leave no sign of my passing, yet always alert for a place to hide. By now they had found my fire, and were on my trail.

My feet were beginning to bleed again. I heard the cry of an eagle that was no eagle, and the cry came from where no eagle would be. One of them had found some sign I'd left and was calling the others.

They would find me now, for they could scatter out and pick up what sign I'd left. I was too slow, too tired, and the going was too rough for me not to make mistakes.

Suddenly, there was no place to go. There'd been no trail. I'd just been following the lines of least resistance, and now the mountainside broke sharply off and I stood on the brink of a cliff with a deep pool of water lying thirty feet below. I could hear water falling somewhere near, but the surface below was unruffled and clear. There was no hesitation in me.

This far I had come, and there could be no thought of turning back. So I dropped my gear into the water, and feet first, I jumped.

A moment of falling, then my body struck the water and knifed into it. There was intense cold. I went down, down, and then as I was coming up my head bumped something and it was the quiver of arrows I'd made. A few yards away was the bow. Gathering them up, I swam for the only shore there was, a narrow white-sand beach back under the overhang of the cliff from which I'd jumped.

No more than four feet long and three wide, it was still a place where I could crawl up and rest. As I neared it I found my spear and the hide with my few belongings in it floating near. After I'd beached the bow and arrows, I recovered them and returned to the beach.

Stretching out on that beach meant putting my feet

in the water, and that was just what I did. That sandy strip was completely invisible from anyone not on the surface of the water, for the pool was rimmed around with smooth rock edges, and none of them seemed to be less than six feet above the water. Even if the Indians circled and got on the rocks opposite they could not see into my hiding place. Their eyes could touch only the water or the rock above me.

Nobody was likely to find me here, but the question was, and it was an almighty big question, how was I going to to get out?

I'd no food left and not much strength, but for the moment I was safe. So I curled up on the sand, pulled the remnants of my hides over me and went to sleep.

And in my sleep I dreamed that I heard a sound of horses, the whimper of a dog or wolf, and the sound of falling water.

When I awakened it was a long time later. I was cold, shivering cold, and the water was gray with late evening. There was a waterfall near . . . not that it mattered.

This was one I wasn't going to get out of.

Galloway, where are you?

Chapter V

"There's a town," Shadow said, "or what passes for a town."

"Flagan don't know nothing about a town. When he taken out he was stark naked an' running his heart out, but if I know Flagan he'll take to the hills. There's places to hide and a better chance of rustling some grub."

"Nevertheless, he's apt to come upon some tracks, and if he follows them he'll find some prospector's camp or a ranch."

"Ranch?"

"They're coming in. The Dunn outfit have laid claim to a wide stretch of range and they're bringing in cattle." Shadow rode around a tree, pulling up to let Galloway ride abreast. "There's some others, too."

"There's room for all."

"Not if you listen to the Dunns. They're a tough lot. From Kansas."

There was the shadow of a trail, long unused. It wound among the rocks and boulders, following the contour of the land. Under the trees it was shadowed and still. Occasionally they drew up to give their horses a breather, for the altitude was high.

"I was talking with an old Ute," Shadow commented,

"and showed him a picture of the castle where I was born. He said there were bigger castles back in the mountains."

"Castles?"

"Big houses," he said, "bigger than any dozen houses he had ever seen, bigger than twice that many, he claimed."

"You'd never guess it. Not in this country. He was probably tellin' you a tall tale."

"Maybe."

Hours later they came down off the mesa into a wide, grassy valley. Almost at once they saw tracks. A dozen riders on shod horses had passed, and not too long before.

Nick Shadow drew up and studied the tracks. Then he looked north in the direction they had gone. "Some of that Dunn outfit," he said. "Stay away from them, Sackett. They're trouble."

"Isn't likely I'll run into them." They mounted a ridge as Galloway spoke and he pointed off to the west. "River over there?"

"The Mancos. Mesa Verde is just beyond. That's where the old Indian told me the castles could be found. Someday I'm going to ride over and have a look."

After a moment Shadow added, "You'd best not hope too much. Your brother didn't have much chance."

"He's a tough man. He's had his tail in a crack before this."

"If I know him he's a comin', and somehow or other he'll keep himself alive. Up to us to find him, no matter how long. No Sackett ever left another in a bind. Leastways, none from my part of the country."

They had turned eastward, and high upon the right, but back from where they rode, the mountains lifted, bold peaks, their rugged flanks streamered with snow, forested almost to the top. They rode cautiously, knowing it was Ute country but also that the Dunns were here.

"I've met none of them," Shadow said, "but they've

a name for being a quarrelsome lot. Rocker Dunn killed
a man over near Pagosa Springs a year back, and they
say he'd killed a couple in Kansas before they came
west. There's talk that several of them rode with Quantrill."

"Where's that town?"

"South of us. East and south. It lies over close to the
La Plata. They've called it Shalako after one of the
Kachinas."

Galloway was thinking of Flagan. Back in those
mountains somewhere he was fighting to keep alive . . .
if he was alive. Without weapons, in a rugged country
where the only humans he found were apt to be enemies, his chances of survival depended upon himself
and his own energies.

They had grown up together, fighting each other's
battles, working together, struggling together, and no
man could know another so well as Galloway knew
Flagan. He knew what Flagan must do to survive because he knew what he would do. And there was no
easy way.

Flagan would be struggling for every mouthful of
food, thinking, conniving, planning. And he would be
working his way north, staying with the kind of country
where he could find a living, and slowly moving toward
the destination for which they had set out.

Shalako lay on the flat with a backdrop of trees and
towering mountains. The flat was green, dotted with
clumps of oak brush, and the metropolis itself was com-
posed of three buildings, two short stretches of boardwalk, one log cabin, a dugout, and several outbuildings
of obvious intent.

"Now look at that," Nick Shadow commented. "It
shows you how fast this country is growing. This town
has increased one-third since I saw it only a few
months ago. Somebody built a barn."

"Livery stable, looks like."

"Well, what more do you want? A saloon, a general store, and a livery stable. That's enough for any town."

"And looks like there's folks in town," Sackett commented. "Four, five horses in front of the saloon, and a buckboard yonder by the store. Business is boomin'."

"They're ruining the country," Shadow agreed. "A year or two ago a man could ride a hundred miles through here and not see anybody, or even hear anybody but the Indians who shot at him. Now look at it. You can hardly walk without falling over people.

"And by the way," he added, as he drew up before the saloon, "that's a Rocking D brand . . . the Dunn outfit."

They swung down, whipped the dust from their clothes, two tall men. Nick Shadow, man of the world, educated, refined, and immaculate . . . not even the long dusty ride had robbed him of that appearance. And Galloway Sackett, in a buckskin coat, a dark blue shirt, shotgun-fringed chaps and boots. On his head a black, flat-crowned hat. He wore his gun tied down, and carried a Bowie knife at his belt. The fact that he had another one, an Arkansas toothpick with a long slender blade, was not obvious. It was suspended between his shoulderblades, the haft within easy grasp below his shirt collar. This was a Tinker-made knife.

Tying their horses they crossed the boardwalk and entered the saloon. Outside it had a false front, behind it a peaked roof, and inside there was no ceiling, just the heavy beams overhead.

There was a long bar, a dozen tables, and chairs. The bartender was a broad-faced man with corn yellow hair, massive forearms resting on the bar. At the end of the bar was a wiry old man with a thin face and high cheekbones, in buckskins.

At a table were three men, obviously cowhands.

"Rye," Shadow said, "for two."

The bartender reached down for a bottle without taking the other arm off the bar and came up with the bottle and two glasses. He put the glasses down and poured, all with his left hand.

Galloway glanced at him thoughtfully, his eyes crinkling at the corners. "Good country around here," he said, speaking to Shadow. "I can see why Tell liked it."

"Tell?" The bartender asked. "You don't mean Tell Sackett?"

"I do mean him," Galloway said. "You know him?"

"Sure do . . . and a good man, too. You mean to say he's been in this country?"

"Several years back. Fact is, Tyrel rode through here one time, too. He'd taken off and was riding around the country, before he got married. And his pa was here long before that, back around 1840."

One of the men at the table, a pugnacious, curly-haired boy of about Galloway's age turned sharply around. "1840? There was nobody here that early."

"My uncle," Galloway said, "was a mountain man. He came down from the north with some other trappers, hunting beaver peltries. He described all of this country to us."

"As a matter of fact," Shadow commented, "there were many here earlier than that. Rivera was up here as early as 1769, and Father Escalante traveled right through here when he was looking for a trail to Monterey, in California."

The young man looked sullen. "I never heard of that. I don't believe it."

"Your privilege," Shadow said. "I realize that education is hard to come by in this part of the country."

The young man had started to turn back to his table. Now he turned sharply around. "What do you mean by that? You sayin' I got no education?"

Nick Shadow smiled. "Of course not. I assumed you were a rather bright young man, and you assumed I was mistaken about Rivera and Escalante. No doubt we were both mistaken."

Shadow turned his back on him, and Galloway said

to the bartender, who was trying to hide a smile. "I'm hunting my brother. He got away from the 'Paches away down south of here and headed into the mountains. He'd be in mighty bad shape. Have you heard anything of such a man?"

"No. And I would have heard, I'm sure. There aren't many people around here. There's the Dunn outfit you were just talking to, and there's Lute Pitcher ... he's got a place a couple of miles over in the hills beyond the river."

"If he shows up, lend a hand. I'll stand good for anything he wants."

The curly-headed man looked around. He had the feeling he had been made a fool of and it rankled. "An' who'll stand good for you?"

Galloway Sackett smiled. "Just me. I think that's enough."

"I don't think it is," the curly-haired one said, "I don't think that's enough at all."

"It is for me," the bartender said calmly. "Sackett is a respected name." And then he added, "Curly, I'd let it alone if I were you."

Curly Dunn got to his feet. "You ain't me, and I don't think much of the name of Sackett." He put his gaze on Galloway. "You want to make something out of that?"

Galloway grinned. "When I do, you'll be the first to know."

He turned to Shadow. "Shall we ride?"

They started for the door, and Curly Dunn shouted after them. "If you're thinkin' of land in this country, you'd better think again. This here is Dunn country!"

Galloway turned. "Are you Dunn?"

"You're durned tootin' I am!"

"Glad to hear it. I'm just beginning." He went out and let the door swing to behind him.

Crossing the street to the general store they entered, buying what supplies they needed. The owner of the store was a slender young man, loose-jointed and friendly.

"My first business," he said. "Pa, he doesn't think I can cut the mustard, but he offered to set me up. Well, I'd saved some, and the rest I borrowed under my own name. I plan to succeed without his help.

"Not," he added, "that there's trouble between us. It's just that I wanted to make it without his help." He grinned. "All I need is more customers."

"We're moving into this country," Galloway said. "We mean to run cattle."

Johnny Kyme glanced at him. "Have you talked to the Dunns about that? They say this is Dunn country."

"We met Curly over yonder," Galloway said dryly. "He sort of led us to believe they figured thataway, but we sort of left the thought with him that we figured to stick around."

Galloway explained about Flagan. "If he shows up, give him whatever he wants. It's good."

They made camp that night in a hollow alongside the rushing waters of the La Plata, with a scattering of aspen about them.

When they had their blankets spread Galloway pulled off his boots and placed them carefully beside him and within easy reach. "I take it kindly, Nick, that you've come along with me."

"I like to ride lonesome country. It's built in me, I guess."

"You born in a castle, and all, I'd figure you for the big towns."

"It wasn't my castle, Sackett. My father owned it and had the title. My mother was the daughter of a younger son who had gone off to sea, lost a leg in a sea battle and came back to set himself up as a woodworker.

"My father had two legitimate sons who looked nothing like him, nor acted it, either. I was his image. His wife met me outside the town once where I was exercising a horse for a man. She asked me to leave

the country. My mother had passed on, and I'd no
taste for woodworking, and she explained to me that I
was too much like her husband not to cause comment.
She said she loved her husband, and she offered to give
me a good sum of money if I'd leave.

"Well, I'd been wanting just that, though doubtful
if I'd ever get it. I'd gone to good schools, but had no
taste for business. So I thanked her, took the money
and came to America.

"I've never told anyone else that, and probably
never will again."

"How about your grandpa?"

"He hated to see me go, but he would have done
the same. I'd have come to nothing there, unless it was
trouble. I wrote to him, sent him money when I had
it. He died a few years ago. The countess wrote and
explained, asking if I wished to come back. One of her
sons had been killed when he was thrown from a horse.
Another got in trouble and left the country, and the
third was not a well men."

"You could go back."

Shadow nodded. "She said my father would make
me legitimate, which might mean I'd inherit. I'm no
longer cut out for it, Sackett. This is my country. Be-
sides, I'd have trouble back east. There was a little
affair in Missouri, a corpse and cartridge occasion . . .
his family was prominent and they would like to find
me."

Neither man spoke for some time, and Shadow
smoked in silence, then put out his pipe and crawled
into his blankets.

"Sackett," Shadow said suddenly, "you've got to see
the high country around here to believe it. There is
nothing more fantastically beautiful. There are towering
peaks, valleys no white man has ever seen, and streams
that run to God knows where. I've seen the Alps and
the Pyrenees, but there's nothing anywhere like these
mountains."

Galloway was silent. Somewhere out in these mountains, perhaps even within a few miles, Flagan was fighting for his life, for his very existence. Slowly he began once more, trying to picture in his brain what must have been happening.

Flagan was a good runner, and he was always in excellent shape. He would have made good time, gotten enough of a lead so they would have a hard time catching up. Food would be harder to come by, but in the mountains they had often rustled their own food.

Somehow Flagan would survive. He must survive.

Chapter VI

For just awhile I lay there shivering in the cold. It was in that last hour before dawn, judging by the few stars I could see. My muscles were stiff and sore, and my feet hurt. I pulled myself painfully to a sitting position and took a slow look around my little island.

The only sound was the rustle of falling water, just loud enough to make it hard to hear anything else that might be stirring around. And then, far off over the mountains, I heard the deep rumble of thunder.

The last thing I wanted right now was a rain storm, me without any clothes, and cold as all get out. Worst of all, I seemed to be trapped in this place and from the looks of the cave walls around me the water in here sometimes rose several feet higher than I could stand. It didn't even have to rain right here to make trouble for me. The water coming down that waterfall I could hear would pour into this basin.

Time to time in my life I'd come up against trouble, but this here seemed about the worst. And my strength was drained by the poor food I'd had, and the beating I'd taken from both the Indians and the wilderness. I'd been bad off before, but at least I'd been out on solid ground where I could travel and maybe rustle a bite to eat. I'd gotten away from the Indians but I'd jumped right into a trap.

Thunder growled deep in the far-off canyons, and I turned my head and began a slow, inch-by-inch check of this place in which I was trapped.

I was on that small bit of sandy beach against the back wall of an overhang that seemed to be of solid rock. From where I sat I could see no break in the wall of the bowl into which I'd jumped, although as water poured into the basin, there must be a way for it to get out.

Finally, I slipped off into the water. Once in the water I was warmer than on the beach, and slowly I swam out into the open air. The rocky edge above me was only a rough six feet above the water, but the wall was sheer, polished by water and worn smooth. Here and there were cracks in the walls, but they were vertical, and there was no way I could see that I could hang on until I could catch hold with the other hand.

The largest one started a good four feet up the wall, and although I jumped a couple of times from the water my fingers wouldn't hold in the slippery crack, so I swam back and stretched out on the sand, just about all in.

Twice more I swam around that pool, trying to find a way out, but my only chance was that crack. Each time I went back to the beach I rested a little longer, for the days of scant food and struggling to cross the country and stay alive had about worn me out. Still, I always told myself, there was nothing a man couldn't get out of if he was sober and didn't panic, so I settled down to think.

The water I'd heard falling wasn't much of a fall, but the rock over which it fell was higher than the place from which I'd jumped, and the rocks were worn smooth.

It began to rain.

First there were scattered big drops, then a steady downpour that freckled the water about me. For awhile

I just lay still, trying to get up energy to try again, and the falling water kind of lulled me to sleep. When I opened my eyes I was shaking with a chill and the water in that basin had raised by at least an inch.

Cold and shivering, I studied the walls again, but always I came back to that crack.

The bottom was a good four feet above the water, and the wall below it was smooth as silk. That crack was maybe four inches wide at the top, but it tapered down to nothing. If a man could have gotten up high enough to get both hands into it with his fingers pulling against opposite edges he might have worked himself to the top . . . he might have.

Toward the bottom there wasn't room to even get one finger into that crack, and I couldn't pull myself up with one finger, anyway.

There didn't seem to be any way out of this fix I'd gotten myself into, and I went back and stretched on the sand again. Seemed to me there was less of it, and the rain was falling steadily.

If I could just find something to wedge into that crevice to give myself a handhold . . . but there was nothing. Of a sudden, I thought of finding a stick, only there were no sticks, and my spear wasn't strong enough to hold my weight even if the crack was deep enough to thrust it in, which it wasn't.

If only there was something. . . . There was!

My fist.

If I could jump high enough out of the water to wedge my doubled-up fist in that crack I could hang by it. If I opened my hand I'd slide right back in the water, but if I could keep my fist closed I could muscle myself up high enough to wedge the other fist crossways in the crack, and then I could grab for the rim.

Something warned me that I had better try. The water running off the mountain in this rain had not yet reached the pool, but it would soon start pouring in from branch streams and runoff gullies, and I'd be forced to swim until I could swim no longer. My little beach would be covered within minutes.

Also, my strength was slipping away. I'd had nothing to eat, and much of my strength had been used up in running, climbing, struggling for life and for food. If this failed there was no other way, so it had to work.

Swimming across the basin I looked up at the crack, so close above me. Now when I was a youngster I'd managed to lunge pretty high out of the water many times in batting a gourd around the old swimming hole. This time I not only had to get about half my body out of the water but I had to wedge my fist in that narrow crack.

First I carried my spear close to the side and threw it atop the wall. Next I threw up my bow and the quiver of arrows.

On my first attempt I succeeded in hitting the wall and bruising myself. On the second my arm went high and my closed fist caught in the crack.

Slowly, flexing my muscles, I lifted my body. It was like chinning myself with one hand, something I'd rarely tried, but my body did come up out of the water and I got my other fist into the crack, but crossways as the crack was wider there. Another lift and I got my other hand on the edge. Pulling myself up, I flopped over on the rocky edge and lay still, the rain pounding on my back.

After awhile, shaking with cold and exhaustion, I got my feet under me, recovered my weapons and started into the woods. That night, cowering among the pine needles, without even the elk hide to cover me, I shivered alone and cold.

How much can a man endure? How long could a man continue? These things I asked myself, for I am a questioning man, yet even as I asked the answers were there before me. If he be a man indeed, he must always go on, he must always endure. Death is an end to torture, to struggle, to suffering, but it is also an end to warmth, light, the beauty of a running horse, the smell of damp leaves, of gunpowder, the walk of a woman when she knows someone watches . . . these things, too, are gone.

In the morning I would have a fire. In the morning I would find food.

The rain fell steadily, and in my huddle under the bushes the big drops came through and rolled coldly down my spine and down my chest.

Stiff and cold, I crept out in the gray dawn. The rain had stopped but the ground was soggy under my feet. Wearing only moccasins and a breech clout I hunted for roots. Starting across a clearing I suddenly heard a rush of movement and looked up in time to be struck by a horse's shoulder and knocked rolling.

Desperately, I tried to get up, to call out, but the wind had been knocked out from me.

A voice said, "That's no Indian! Curly, that's a white man!"

"Aw, what difference does it make? Leave him lay!"

It taken me a minute to get up and I called after him. "Help me. Get me to a ranch or somewhere. I'll—"

The rider called Curly spun his horse and came back at a run. He had a coil of rope in his hand and he was swinging it for a blow. Trying to step aside my feet skidded on the wet leaves and the horse hit me again, knocking me into the brush. Curly rode away laughing.

After a long while I got my knees under me and crawled to where my arrows were. The bowstring was wet and useless, but the spear might get me something. First I needed a fire. In a hollow near the river, I broke the dried-out twigs that were lowest on the tree trunks, gathered some inner bark from a deadfall and rigged a small shelter to keep the raindrops from my fire.

With my stone knife I cut out a little hollow in a slab of wood broken loose when a tree fell, then a notch from the hollow to the edge.

Powdering bark in my hands I fed the dust into the hollow, then used my bow and a blunt arrow-shaft to start the fire. It took several minutes of hard work to get a smoke and then a spark, but I worked on a bit, then managed to blow the spark into life. At last I had a fire.

It is times such as this that show a man how much the simple things like food and warmth can mean. Slowly my fire blazed up, and the first warmth in a long time began to work its way into my stiff, cold muscles.

Everything was damp. I'd nothing to cover my nakedness, but the fire brought a little warmth to me, and just having it made me feel better. My feet were in bad shape again, although not so bad as at first, and the bruises from the beating I'd taken showed up in great blotches over my hide. I huddled there by the fire, shivering, wishing for food, for warmth, for a blanket.

It was unlikely any wild game would stir during the rain, so I must wait it out or try to find what roots there might be, but looking from where I sat I saw nothing I could eat. Yet I had lived long enough to know that nothing lasts forever, and men torture themselves who believe that it will. The one law that does not change is that everything changes, and the hardship I was bearing today was only a breath away from the pleasures I would have tomorrow, and those pleasures would be all the richer because of the memories of this I was enduring.

It was not in me to complain of what had happened. A man shares his days with hunger, thirst and cold, with the good times and the bad, and the first part of being a man is to understand that. Leastways, I had two hands, two feet and two eyes, and there were some that lacked these things. The trouble was that I wasn't feeling quite right . . . I'd a sense of things being unreal, and of sickness coming on, and that scared me something sinful.

To be sick, alone, and in the woods, with the weather damp and cold . . . it was not a thing to favor the mind.

Of a sudden I was sweating, out there in the cold and rain, I was sweating where a short time before I'd been chilled and shaking. I burrowed down into the pine needles and leaves, and fortunate it was that here where I'd stopped the carpet was thick.

I'd stick out a hand from time to time to put something on the fire, scared of the time when it would be used up around me and I'd have to get out and go to hunting. There were willows near, and I peeled back the bark to get at the inner bark, which was good for fevers, and chewed some.

Along in there somewhere I sort of passed out. There was a time when I put a stick or two on the fire, added some leaves for lack of anything else.

Once I thought I heard a horse coming, and it was in my mind that somebody called out to me, but I don't know if I answered. My head felt light and my mouth was dry, and I was cold . . . cold.

I've heard folks say that if you're down in a dark hole and you look up you can see the stars, even by day. Well, I looked up and saw a face looking into mine with wide eyes and lips parted, and it was like looking up out of that hole and seeing a star. Anyway, it was the last I saw for some time.

We never had much in the mountains. The fixings around the house were such as Ma contrived, or Pa when he was not too tired from work. Nothing fancy, just a few little things like curtains at the window, and flowers on the table, and Ma when she swept the floor and could keep us boys off it for awhile, she traced patterns in the dirt floor like you'd find on the finest carpets. Ma was good at that, and she liked things nice.

About the best we could manage was to keep them clean.

You don't make much on a sidehill farm in Tennessee. The country is right beautiful, and that is where you have to find what beauty there is, there, and in the singing. Most mountain folks sing. They sing songs learned from their grandfathers or other elders, and sometimes they change the tunes to fit the day, and change the words even more.

You get a hankering for nice things if there's much to you. It seems to me that first a man tries to get shelter and food to eat, but as soon as he has that he tries to find beauty, something to warm the heart and the mind, something to ease the thoughts and make pleasurable the sitting in the evening. About all we had was the open fire. It was the thing we set store by. Ma, she was too busy knitting and sewing just to keep us covered to have much time for fixing.

Opening my eyes like I done, in that bedroom with lacy curtains to the windows and a handsome patchwork quilt over me, I thought I'd sure come to in the house of some rich folks, or in heaven mostly, although I never did rightly know whether they'd have patchwork quilts. She set store by them, and she was always a saving of odds and ends she might use toward one. She never did get to make it. Pneumonia came too soon, and pneumonia to mountain folk far from doctors is nothing to feel good about.

There I lay, a long tall mountain boy in such a bed as I'd never seen, looking up at a painted plank ceiling . . . well, maybe it was whitewashed.

I turned my head and saw a dresser set against the wall with a mirror over it, and there was a small table with a pitcher and a washbasin. In a dish alongside the basin was a bar of soap. These here were surely well-to-do folks.

When I tried to set up I felt giddy, but the first thing I saw was that I was wearing a flannel nightshirt. I'd had a nightshirt one time, quite awhile back, but they were scarce. I was seventeen years old before I owned a pair of socks. We boys just shoved our feet down into boots.

We never had much, Galloway and me. First big money we made was on the buffalo range. We were shooters, me and him, and mostly we hit what we shot at. Back in the high-up hills a body didn't have enough ammunition to go a-wasting of it. When you shot at something you'd better hit it. Which led to our being good at stalking and tracking because we had to get close up before we chanced a shot. And if the animal was wounded and ran off, we had to track it down, for the needing of the meat and not wishing to leave any crittur to suffer in the woods.

That money we made on the buffalo range, that went to squaring Pa's debts, of which he'd left a few with men who trusted him. We never taken a trust lightly. It was a matter of deep honor, and a debt owed was a debt to be paid.

I lay there in that big bed, just a-staring up at the white ceiling and wondering how come I was here in this place.

There was a door opening to a sort of closet and in it I could see women's fixings and some man's shirts and pants. I could also see a holster with a gun in it. Gave me a comfort to have it near.

Footsteps were coming down the hall and then the door opened and a man came in. He was a square-shouldered man with a mustache and wearing a white shirt. He looked down at me.

"Awake are you? You've had a bad time of it, man."

"I reckon. How long have I been here?"

"Six . . . seven days. My daughter found you. How she got you on her horse I will never know."

I was tired. I closed my eyes a minute, thinking how lucky I was.

"You had pneumonia," he said. "We didn't think we could pull you through. At least, I didn't. Maighdlin, she never did give up."

"Where is this place?"

"It's on Cherry Creek, about six or seven miles from where you were picked up." He sat down in the chair he pulled up. "I am John Rossiter. What happened to you?"

It took me a couple of minutes to think that over, and then I explained about us hunting land, the Jicarillas, and my escape. I also told the part about the rider who wouldn't lend me a hand. "They called him Curly."

Just as I said that a mighty pretty girl stepped into the room, her face flushed and angry. "I don't believe that!" she said sharply. "You must have been out of your head."

"Could be, ma'am," I said politely, not being one to argue with a lady. "Only that horse surely hit me a wallop to be part of something imaginary. And they sure enough called him Curly."

"Did you see any tracks, Meg?"

She hesitated, her eyes bright and angry. Reluctantly, she said, "Yes, I did. There were some tracks. Two horses, I think. Possibly three. But it wasn't Curly Dunn! It couldn't have been!"

"Maybe I was wrong," I said. "I didn't intend to hurt your feelings, ma'am."

"If I were you, Meg," Rossiter said, "I'd give that a good deal of thought. There's a lot of talk about Curly, and not much of it is good."

"They're jealous!" she said pertly. "Jealous of him because he's so handsome, and of the Dunns because they've taken so much land. I don't believe any of it."

"Mr. Rossiter," I said, "if you could lend me some clothes, a horse and a gun, I'll be on my way. I don't like to saddle myself on you folks."

"Don't be silly!" Meg said sharply. "You're not well enough to travel. Why, you look half-starved!"

"I can make out, ma'am. I don't want to stay where I'm not wanted."

"You be still," she said. "I'll get you some soup."

When she had gone, Rossiter hesitated a moment

and then asked, "This man called Curly? Can you describe him?"

"Big, strong young feller, rosy color to his cheeks, brown wavy hair and he favors them big Mexican spurs. He was riding a handsome gray horse . . . no cowhand's horse."

"Yes, that's Curly." Rossiter got up suddenly. "Damn it, man, don't ever try to raise a daughter in a country where men are scarce! I've heard talk about Curly Dunn. He's hard on his horses, and he's a quarrelsome man who's forever picking fights. Most people are afraid of him because of Rocker."

"Rocker Dunn?" I knew that name, as a good many did. Rocker Dunn was said to have ridden with Quantrill, and for a time he'd been a known man down in the Cherokee Nation and in East Texas. He was tough and strong and had the name of being a dead shot who would sooner be shooting than talking.

"That's the one. You know of him?"

"Yes, sir. I've heard the name."

"Sackett," Rossiter said, "I want you to stay on until you're strong again. When you're ready to go I'll outfit you. We don't have much, but we'll share what we have."

He pointed toward the closet. "There's a six-shooter in there if you should need it. It is an old gun but a good one and I trust you'll use it with judgment."

After he'd gone I lay there awhile, just a-thinking. Seems we Sacketts were never going to be shut of trouble. We had started for this wild, new country to build us a home, and it was country like nobody ever saw before. It was mountain country, which suited us, but the mountains were giants compared to what we'd been used to. Clingman's Dome was a mighty beautiful peak, but would be lost in the shadow of most of those around me.

Running water, lakes, aspen, pines, spruce, and so much fish and game the stuff fairly jumped at a man . . . there was hay in the meadows, flowers on the slopes, and timber for the cutting. It was our kind of country, and here we Sacketts would stay.

I eased myself out of bed and started to stand up, but felt giddy of a sudden and sat down, my head all aswim. I'd have to take it easy. I'd have to wait it out. There was no place in this country for a man who couldn't walk tall down the trails or sit a saddle where the long wind blows.

The pistol was one of those made in Texas during the War Between the States. It was a Dance & Park percussion pistol, .44 calibre, that had been worked over to handle Colt cartridges. Somebody had worked on that gun who knew what he was doing. It had balance and felt right to a man's hand. The pistol was loaded and the loops in the belt were filled. I taken it down and hung it by the bed.

A good gun is a thing to have, and a body never knows when he'll need it.

There's a saying that when guns are outlawed, only the outlaws will have guns.

Chapter VII

It was a mark of my weakness that I was almighty glad to get back into bed, and I dozed off after awhile and only awakened when Meg Rossiter came into my room with a tray to put on the bedside table.

Now this was a new thing for me. I'd never been waited on much. Not since Ma died. Or when I paid for it in some roadside eating place.

This here was something, to set up in bed with pillows propped behind, and good food there for you. "Ma'am, you could plumb spoil a man, doin' for him like this."

"You're sick," she said, and I figured there was a mite of edge to her tone. She didn't set so much store by me since I'd told what happened on the trail. But I'd no idea she was sweet on this Curly fellow . . . and it was too bad. Any man who would do to me what he'd done had something rotten inside.

All right. He had no cause to help me, but he'd no cause to come back and knock me down, either. The first time might have been an accident, although I was no longer sure of that. The second time was not.

"I know you don't think much of me, ma'am, and as soon as I'm able I'll ride out of here. You'll be shut of me."

"But not what you said! You'll leave that behind! You'll leave it with Pa!"

"I only told the truth, ma'am, and when I spoke I had no idea you was sweet on him."

"I'm not! I'm not what you said! You probably think if Curly were out of the way I'd look at you!"

"No, ma'am," I said honestly, "I think nothing of the kind. I know I'm a homely man, ma'am, just a long tall mountain boy. Now Galloway . . . he's my brother . . . womenfolk pay him mind, but none of them ever looked twice at me, and I've come not to expect it."

She looked at me suddenly, as if seeing me for the first time. "You're not homely," she said. "Maybe you aren't handsome, but you're not homely, either."

"Thank you, ma'am. I reckon I decided long ago that I'd have to run in single harness. I like the high, lonesome country, so maybe it fits. Nobody ever wanted a home more than me, and nobody ever had one less, least it was Galloway. Gals like the high-spirited, high-headed kind, I've noticed. If they can break them to harness they aren't at all what the gal wanted in the beginning, and if she can't break them they usually break her. But that's the way of it."

She went back into the other room, wherever it was, and I ate my soup. It was good soup, and I thought how I'd lied in my voice if not in my heart. I did so think about her. When a big, homely man like me has a woman do for him it softens him up, and me being lonely like so much of the time, it was just natural I'd think of how fine it would be, but there's no harm in thinking, and I knew all the time it was impossible. Still, I wished it was somebody else than that Curly.

I wished it was anybody else than Curly.

After I'd eaten, I slept. What awakened me I don't know, but it must have been the sound of horses' hoofs in the ranch yard. Rising up on one elbow, I listened and heard voices.

Reaching over to that holster I drew out that Dance & Park pistol and brought it back into bed with me, taking it under the covers and alongside my right leg. With a man like Curly Dunn you have no idea, and after what he'd done I had a hunch that had he met me out on the trail alone he would have killed me . . . just for the hell of it.

With his friend along I guess he just didn't want to be that ornery. Nobody looks on cold-blooded killing with favor, not even those liable to do it themselves . . . a body never knows when he'll be the victim with a man like that.

Anyway, it gave me a right comforting feeling to have that old six-shooter under my hand.

There was talk in the other rooms that I could hear vaguely, talk and laughter and some singing. Meg was playing a banjo and singing soft and low, so I could not hear the words. It would have been a good sound to go to sleep by, only I daren't. Soon or late she was going to tell him about the man she found alongside the trail, and he would come to look.

Suddenly I heard footsteps and then the door opened. Curly stood there, looking across the room at me. I was setting up.

"They were fools to take you in," he said. "They've no idea who you are."

"Neither do you," I said. "But they're good folks, who'd help a man who was hurt . . . not ride him down."

He chuckled, but it was a mean kind of humor. "You looked funny," he said, "topplin' over thataway. Like a rag doll."

He started toward me, dropping his hand to his gun. "You're the kind who might commit suicide," he said thoughtfully, "a man as bad off as you are. It wouldn't surprise anybody."

"It would surprise my brother Galloway," I said, "and the rest of the Sacketts. But don't you worry none. I'm not figurin' on it."

"But with a little help?"

He meant it, too. There was a cruel streak in the man, a mean, cruel streak. He taken another step toward me and then almost by accident his eyes fell on the empty holster hanging to the bedpost.

It stopped him.

That and my right hand under the covers. Did I have the gun? He didn't know, but I could see him begin to sweat. The beads just stepped out on his forehead like water had been thrown at him.

He looked at me, and toward the blanket where my right hand was hidden, and I could just see him wondering if I'd draw that gun from under the covers in time, so I said, "Now no man in his right mind draws a gun from under blankets when he can shoot right through them."

He looked at me, his eyes all hot and bright, the sweat still on him, his fear fighting with his greed to kill or maim. "You've got a gun?"

"Have I?" I grinned at him. "It's a good question, isn't it? I didn't have one out on the trail, bein' stark naked as I was, but Mr. Rossiter might have given me one."

"He wouldn't be such a fool. You might murder them all."

"Maybe he thinks they're in less danger from me than from you."

That hit him. He liked being what he was but he did not like having it known, or guessed.

"What's the matter?" I asked. "Was it Rocker's name that got to you? You probably decided you could kill more men than he could . . . only Rocker generally shoots them standing up. Or so I've heard."

He kind of drew back. He had decided he did not like the odds. He might have tried it, at that, and then tried to convince the Rossiters it had been suicide. Such men often believe the impossible because it suits them to believe, or because they have big ideas of themselves.

Just then we heard the click of heels and then Meg was in the room, her pa right behind her.

"Oh! Here you are! I went to put fudge on the dish and start some coffee and when I got back you were gone."

"He came back to pay his respects, ma'am," I said dryly. "It was the only polite thing to do."

She shot him a quick glance, then looked hard at me. Curly Dunn looked as bland and innocent as a newborn baby, but I expect that was how he always looked. Only when he glanced at me his eyes took on that greasy look.

When they had gone Rossiter remained behind. "What happened?" he demanded.

I shrugged. "Nothing. Nothing at all."

Rossiter's eyes went to the empty holster, then to my right hand under the covers. "You're a careful man," he said.

"My grandpa," I said, "lived to be ninety-four. It was a caution to us all."

We talked the evening away, mostly of cows and ranching, Indians and the like, and all the while I was learning about this country, the prettiest I'd ever seen.

"In the country north of Shalako," he said, "there's high mountain parks the like of which you've never seen. Running streams everywhere, waterfalls, lost canyons, and good feed for stock. I've seen outcrops of coal, and there are stories that the old Spanish men mined for gold up there."

"I'll be riding out," I said, "but I'll be coming back . . . with Galloway."

He glanced at me. "Curly says he's met your brother. That Galloway Sackett backed down from him."

"Galloway," I told him, "hasn't any back-up in him. He probably didn't figure it was the custom of the country to kill somebody that isn't dry behind the ears yet."

He left me finally, and I eased down into the bed and stretched out. It felt good, real good. I was warm,

I had eaten, and I could rest. Yet I did not let myself fall asleep until I heard Curly Dunn ride off.

Rossiter had a small operation going for him, a herd of no more than three hundred head, mostly breeding stock, but he was a prosperous man and had come into the country with money. He had no need to sell stock, and could hold off and let the natural increase build his herd. Although I expect he had the notion of picking up a few head when buying was possible. A man with ready cash can often make some good buys of folks who just can't cut the mustard.

He had built a strong five-room house of logs with three good fireplaces, one of them big enough to warm two rooms and which could be fed from both. He had a weather-tight stable and some pole corrals, and he had a dozen head of good horses and two cowhands. In the house he had a Mexican woman for a cook who looked strong enough to handle both of the cowhands in a rough-and-tumble fight. But she could really throw the grub together.

She brought me breakfast in the morning, and then she brought me some clothes. The pants were a might short in the leg as I am two inches above six feet, and the shirt was short in the arm, but it felt good to have civilized clothes on again. They hadn't no spare boots but they did have hide, so I set to work and made myself a pair of moccasins.

Meg stopped by to watch. She set down on the porch beside me whilst I cut them out and shaped them to my feet. "You have done that before?"

"Often. I can make a fair pair of boots, too, given the time."

"Have you?"

"In the Sackett family if a boy wanted boots he made 'em himself. That is, if he was over twelve. Before that we mostly went barefooted. I was sixteen year old before I had me a pair of store-bought shoes. I saved 'em for dancin'."

She hugged her knees and looked at the line of

trees beyond the ranch-yard. "What were the dances like?"

"Well, most often they were at the schoolhouse. Sometimes they'd be in somebody's yard. The word would go out and folks would tell each other, and each would fix up a basket and go. Other times it would just be sort of on the spur, and they'd come from all over.

"Most of the boys weren't so much for dancin' but if they couldn't dance they could hold the girl whilst she did. There'd be a fiddle, sometimes some other instrument, but a fiddle was all anybody expected or needed.

"A lot of courtin' was done at those dances, and a lot of fightin'. Mostly the boys came for the fightin'. Galloway always had some girl who'd set her cap for him, but he paid them no mind. Not serious, anyway.

"Sometimes there'd not be enough for dancin' so we'd set about an' sing. I liked that because I just plain like to sing."

"What are you going to do now?"

"Hunt us a piece of land and go to ranching. I reckon right now the thing to do is head for Shalako and team up with Galloway."

"You'd better be careful. The Dunns will think you're crowding them."

"It's open range, and there's enough for all."

"That isn't what they think, Mr. Sackett. There are six of the Dunn boys, and there's their pa, and they've a dozen or more men who ride for them."

"Well, there's two of us Sacketts. That should make it work out about right. Of course, if need be there's a lot of us scattered around and we set store by our kinfolk."

I completed the moccasins and tried them on. They felt good on my feet, which had healed over, although the skin was still tender.

I looked down at the girl. "Ma'am, you're a right pretty girl, and the man that gets you will be lucky, but don't you go wasting yourself on Curly Dunn. He's as poisonous mean as a rattler."

She sprang to her feet, her face stiff with anger. "Nobody can be nice to you! The first time I try to talk to you you end up by criticizing Curly!"

"If I hadn't been armed last night, he'd have killed me."

"What kind of talk is that? You mean he'd have tried to kill you right in my own house, with Pa and me close by? That's ridiculous!"

"Maybe. He said it would look like suicide. Ma'am, you may hate me for this, but I'd be less than a man if I hadn't told you. That Curly is sick. He's sick in the head. You'd better understand that while there's still time."

Scornfully, she turned from me. "Go away. And I don't care if I ever see you again! Just go away!"

"Yes, ma'am. That's why I told you. Because I am going away and I don't figure to see you again too much, and you and your pa have been almighty kind. I've warned you just like I'd warn folks if there was a hydrophoby wolf in the neighborhood."

I limped to the corral and roped the *grulla* mustang Rossiter had agreed to loan me. I saddled up with the borrowed gear, then went to the house.

Rossiter met me at the door. "Sorry to see you go, boy. If you come back this way, drop in."

"I'll return the outfit soon as I can rustle one. Galloway has a little money. I lost all mine back yonder."

"No hurry." Rossiter stepped down off the porch and lowered his tone. "Sackett, you be careful, riding out of here. I think you have made an enemy."

"If he stays out of my way, I'll stay shut of him. I'm not one to hunt trouble. An' Mr. Rossiter, if you ever need help, you just put your call on a Sackett. You'll get all the help you need, an' quick. You help one of us and you've helped us all. That's the way we figure it."

The *grulla* was a good horse, mountain-bred and

tough. He was a mite feisty there at first but as soon as he found that I intended to stay in the saddle and take no nonsense he headed off down the trail happily enough. He just wanted to settle as to who was boss.

Shalako wasn't far down the road. I kept to the trees, avoiding the trail, and at noontime I watered in the La Plata River a few miles below the town. When the *grulla* was watered I taken it back under the trees and found a place there with sunshine and shadow, with grass around, and a place for me to rest, and I rested while the *grulla* cropped grass.

Fact is, I wasn't up to much, and what lay beyond I did not know. There might be folks at the town that I wanted to see, and some I'd rather fight shy of.

Somehow the thought was in my mind that I was coming home . . . this country felt right to me, and I even liked the name of that town.

Shalako . . . some Indian name, it sounded like.

Then, for awhile, listening to the cropping of grass and the running water, I slept.

Chapter VIII

The town lay off the road with the most beautiful backdrop of mountains you ever did see, and the La Plata was down off the bench and under the trees, hidden from the town, but close by.

Now when I say "town" I mean it western style. In this country we folks call anything a town where people stop. First off there's a stage stop or a store or maybe only a saloon. Out California way there was a town started because a man's wagon broke down and he just started selling whiskey off the tailgate.

Generally towns in this country, like in the old country, began at river crossings or places where the trails crossed. Folks like to stop at rivers, but the smart ones always cross the river first, and then camp. The river might rise up during the night and hold them for days.

London, folks tells me, began at the only good crossing of the river in many miles. At that place there was a gravel bottom. The same thing folks tell me was true of other cities about the world, but how Shalako came to be, I had no idea.

It was mid-afternoon when my mustang ambled up the one street of the town. With the mountains reared up against the sky in the background there were three buildings, two on one side of the street, one on the other. I swung down in front of the saloon and tied my horse, sizing up the place.

Across the street was a general store and as soon as I could round up some cash I figured to go over there and buy myself an outfit, including boots. Meanwhile I'd tackle the saloon.

Now a western saloon wasn't just a place to belt a few. It was a clubroom for the men, a clearing house for information, and often as not more business was done at the bar than anywhere else around. A man could go into a saloon and find out how the trails were, whether the Indians were on the warpath, or just about anything he needed to know. And I needed to know plenty. Mostly where I could find Galloway.

So I pushed past the swinging doors and went in. It was cool and quiet inside. The bar ran across about two-thirds of the end of the room, and by the end of the bar there was a door. That bar was polished and in mighty fine shape. There were a dozen tables, a beat-up music box, and a man leaning over the bar.

"Howdy," I said, "I'm Flagan Sackett. I'm hunting a brother of mine and somebody who'll stake me to a bait of grub."

"Your brother Galloway Sackett?"

"That's the one."

"He and his partner rode off up country. They said to give you whatever you needed, so the grub will be ready. You want a drink?"

"Thanks. I don't shape up to be much of a drinking man, but I'll have it."

Now I didn't shape up to be much of anything right then. Like I said, those clothes I had on fit me a mite too soon. The pants ended above my ankles and the shirt sleeves only came down below my elbows. The shirt was tight across the chest and back, and of course, thin like I was from lack of eating, I looked like the skeleton had come out of the cupboard.

Just then the doors swung open and two men came in—cowhands from somebody's outfit. They wore chaps and they bellied up to the bar and then one of them saw me.

"Look what the cat dragged in," he said. "Mister, next time you swipe somebody's pants you better make sure they fit."

"That would be hard to do," I said, "judging by what I see around. I don't think there's a man-sized pair of pants in the outfit, letting alone the bartender."

One of those gents was a stocky, redheaded gent with square shoulders and freckled hands . . . fists right now. He taken a step toward me and said, "Let's see who fills the biggest pants around here."

"Mister Red," I said, "I'm in no shape for a fight. I've come off the mountain after a most difficult time with Indians and such. You just hold that head of steam for a week or so and I'll take you out and punch your head into shape."

"I think you're yella," he said.

"No," I said, "although I can understand your viewpoint. But I don't aim to give myself none the worst of it and I'm in no shape to fight. Right at this moment I couldn't whip a sick kitten."

The bartender came through the door from the kitchen pushing a tray loaded with grub ahead of him. "Here you go, Sackett," he said. "This'll put meat on your ribs."

That redhead stared at me. "Is your name Sackett? You related to Tyrel?"

"Cousins," I said, "although the only time we ever met was down in the Tonto Basin awhile back. Do you know Tyrel?"

"I know him. He's hell-on-wheels with a gun."

"Runs in the family," I said. "We all take to shooting like we do to girling or eating. Comes natural. I cut my teeth on the butt of a six-gun."

"We had trouble, Tyrel an' me."

"Must not have amounted to much," I said, "that trouble you speak of."

"Why?"

"You're still alive, ain't you? The way I heard it Tyrel don't waste around. When he has a job to do he does it. If I were you I'd forget all about that trouble. And whatever you had in mind here, too. I don't want nothing to take my mind off this grub."

So saying I straddled a chair and cut into that meat. Hungry as I was it could have been an old saddle and I'd have eaten it, stirrups and all.

Red brought his beer over and sat down opposite me. "Truth to tell," he said, "Tyrel could have pinned my ears back, and he didn't. I was tied in with a rough crowd and I was feeling my weight. I never did get nowhere bucking Sacketts."

"Then it's about time you either stayed out of the fights or got in on the right side."

"Which side is yours?"

"One not hunting trouble. We came into this country hunting land. We figure to settle down and raise cows and families. You got anything against that?"

"No . . . but the Dunns might."

Well, I didn't want to talk about it. Seemed to me there'd been too much talk already. What I wanted was some shut-eye, now that I was stowing away this grub. I wanted a rest and then an outfit. I'd need blankets, a poncho, saddlebags, a rifle, and some grub. It was a lot to ask, but no more than I could pay for, given time.

The saloonkeeper left his bar and crossed over to my table with a beer. "Mind if I join you? Name's Berglund."

He was a big, tough-looking man with yellow hair, a wide, battle-scarred face, and massive shoulders, arms and fists. "Glad to have company," I said. "You been here long?"

"Nobody has. I was driftin' through the country, headed west. I suppose I was huntin' gold, and did make a pass at it now and again, but then I came up on this bench and I decided this was there I wanted to stay. The fishing was great and the hunting was even better, so I bought an axe and an adze and built myself a saloon. I figured that was the easiest way to find company.

"In the good months I fish and hunt, and in the winter I sit by the fire and read or talk. I'm a talkative man, Sackett. I like people, and enjoy their company. Nothing like a warm fire when the weather's turning bad to get folks to sit up and talk."

"It's a risk meeting folks," I said. "You never know which one is a danger to you. It's like coming to a crossroads where you pull up and look both ways and your whole life may change if you take the wrong direction. One thing you can be sure of . . . your life wouldn't be the same."

"I don't know," Berglund argued, "I think a man takes trouble with him."

"Well," I said, "I surely didn't want trouble when Curly Dunn first came up on me. He brought it to me. And I'd no idea I'd ever see him again, but when Meg Rossiter taken me home she taken me right into the middle of the target."

When I finished that meal I just sat there for a moment, enjoying the contented feeling that was settling me down. I sorely needed an outfit, but right now I'd no desire to get my feet under me and walk over there. Nor was there pleasure in the thought of pushing my sore feet down into new boots.

"There's folks a-coming in," Berglund said, "most of them prospectors, but there's a few farmers and cattlemen coming, too. This here's a growing land."

"The Dunns come in often?"

"Nearly every day. They spend money, but I don't care for them. And the worst of them isn't Curly, either. He's small calibre compared to Ollie Hammer or Tin-Cup Hone. Tin-Cup got his name from the mining camp they call Tin-Cup. They had a way of running marshals out of town or killing them, and Tin was one of the worst of the lot. Then he ran into Ollie and they teamed up and came down here and signed on to punch cows for Old Man Dunn and his boys. That's a mean lot."

Getting to my feet I thanked him and walked outside. The sun was still bright on the mountains although it would soon be hidden behind them. I walked across the street, limping some, and went into the store.

Galloway had been there before me and told them I might show up, so I outfitted myself with new pants, shirts, underwear, and socks. I looked at the guns but decided to hang onto the old Dance & Park six-shooter. That gun felt lucky to my hand.

When I walked back to the saloon I was toting a full outfit, right down to a brand spanking new Winchester. And you know something? That was the first new gun I'd ever owned. Always before it was some hand-me-down, owned by a half-dozen before me.

Berglund had him a back room and I changed there and got into my new outfit, all but the boots. I set them aside for a time when my feet would be well enough. Then I taken that Winchester and loaded her to the guards. She was a '73, and carried seventeen bullets in the magazine and chamber.

When I came back into the saloon Berglund looked at me and said, "You're all slicked up to go courtin'. Who'll it be? Meg Rossiter?"

"She'd never look twice at me," I said. "But I'll tell you what I want to do. I want to write a letter. You got the makin's?"

So Bergland fixed me up with paper and pen, and then went to stirring up a fire. Fine as it was in the daytime a body could always sleep under a blanket there at Shalako, which suited me.

The letter I wrote was to Parmalee. He was a flatland Sackett, folks of which we'd heard tell but had never met up with until that trouble down in the Tonto Basin when Tyrel and Parmalee Sackett showed up.

He was an educated man. Those flatland Sacketts had money. They were well-off, and Parmalee had been to school and all. It never affected his shooting, though, so I reckon school is a thing to be wished for. Wishing never done me any good.

Parmalee had cattle, and this here was fine grazing land, and Parmalee had something else he'd need. He had nerve.

When I'd finished the letter to Parmalee, telling him of the range, I suddenly had a thought. We were shaping up for trouble with the Dunns, and that was excuse enough to write to Logan.

Now Logan was a Clinch Mountain Sackett, and those boys from Clinch Mountain are rougher than a cob. There were those who called Logan an outlaw, but he was family, and he was handy with a shooting iron.

I wrote to him, too.

Trouble was, the shooting was likely to be over and done with before any of those boys ever got here, unless it was Parmalee, who was down in New Mexico, not far south of the line.

He might make it in time. And of a sudden I had a hunch we'd need him.

This country was shaping up for war.

Chapter IX

Leaving my gear at Berglund's place, I mounted that *grulla* and rode down off the bench into the river bottom of the La Plata. It was very still. There was grass, and everywhere a body looked there were the tall white trunks of the aspen. Stopping at the river I let the mustang drink from the cold water that ran down from the melting snows on the mountains.

Across the stream I went up through the trees beyond. There was a plateau over there with good grass, a few clumps of oak brush here and there, but a fresh, green country lying at the foot of the mountains.

There were pines along the mountain slopes with thick-standing clumps of aspens of a lighter green. The aspen was usually the first tree to grow up after a burn, and the aspen groves provided a lot of food for wildlife.

Riding slowly along the edge of the mountain and up under the trees along the slope, I knew this was my country, this was where I wanted to be. This was the land I'd been looking for and no amount of Dunns would keep me off of it.

I headed back to Shalako.

The first person I saw when I walked into the saloon

was old Galloway, and I never laid eyes on anybody
that looked better.

"You look kind of peaked," he said, grinning at me.
"I declare, the first time I leave you alone you make
out to get yourself killed, or nigh onto it.

"Flagan, this here's Nick Shadow . . . a good friend."

"Howdy."

"My pleasure."

We all sat down together at a table and went over
what had taken place, and we came to agreement on
Curly Dunn. Galloway looked me over mighty curious
when I talked about Meg Rossiter, and I felt myself
flushing. More because he was looking at me than anything else. It was no use him thinking there was ought
between us, nor me thinking it either.

The only thing she wanted from me was distance,
and I had no ache to a shoot-out with Curly Dunn
over a girl that couldn't see me for dust. What I had
to tell them then was about the land I'd seen, and they
agreed.

I taken to Shadow. Galloway and me, we see things
about the same, and anybody I liked he liked and the
other way around. Nick Shadow was a tall, handsome
man but one who had judgment as well as education,
and the two don't always accompany one another. I've
seen some men who were mighty bright in their books
who couldn't tell daylight from dark when it came to
judging men or the condition of things.

Now I hold by the Good Book, but in some ways I
am closer to the Old Testament than the New. I believe
in forgiving one's enemies, but keep your hand on your
gun while you do it, mentally, at least. Because while
you are forgiving him he may be studying ways to get
at you.

I like my fellow man, but I also realize he carried
a good measure of the Old Nick in him and he can
find a good excuse for almost any kind of wrongdoing
or mischief. I wanted no trouble with the Dunns, and
would avoid giving them cause, but at the same time I

had common sense enough to realize they might not feel the same way. A man who starts imagining that others think good because he does is simply out of his mind. I've helped bury a few who did think that way . . . nice, peaceful men who wanted no trouble and made none.

When feeding time comes around there's nothing a hawk likes better than a nice, fat, peaceful dove.

"We can lay claim to land," I said, "but we'll have to have cattle on it. I've written to Parmalee."

"I've got a few head," Shadow said. "We might include them in the drive."

We spent the evening talking about the ranch we wanted, the cattle drive to come, and the future of the country. There was or had been a fort over on the Animas, and Berglund told us there was a house over there if you wanted to call it that. So we were not alone in the country. There was an Irishman named Tim McCluer who had moved into the country and he was getting along with the Utes . . . which showed that it could be done.

McCluer told Berglund that the Utes and the Jicarillas usually got along, so the bunch who had been hunting me were likely to have been renegades, prepared to plunder anyone who crossed their trail. The Indians had men like that as well as the whites.

We stabled our horses in the livery barn and camped in the loft. Falling asleep that night I dreamed of my own outfit, and slept with the smell of fresh hay in my nostrils.

We moved over west of the town, and west of the La Plata, and we made camp there in a grove of aspen, a splendid country spread out before us. We decided we'd all spend some days working on the beginnings of a spread, and after that Nick Shadow would take off for the south to meet Parmalee and to round up his own cattle to join the herd.

"I don't need to tell you boys," he said, "but keep the Dunns in mind. They're a tough, lawless outfit and they won't take lightly to our being here. Especially after both of you have had words with Curly."

First off, we built a corral, and then a lean-to. We built them back into the woods with a screen of trees between us and the open flat. Then we went back into the trees and cut some limbs here and there, and a whole tree yonder to scatter amongst the other trees and make a sort of crude barrier for anybody who tried to come up behind us.

There was nothing that would stop anyone, but nobody could come up through those trees without arousing us.

Galloway and me, we weren't like the usual cowhand, who'd rather take a whipping than do any work that can't be done on a horse. We were both planting boys from the hills, who could plow as straight a furrow as the next man, if need be, so we spaded up a corner of ground, worked over the sod and went down to the store to buy seed. We planted potatoes, carrots, pumpkins and corn, to start. We had no idea how they'd grow, but if they did they'd be a help. Starting a home in a new land is never a bed of roses, but then we didn't come looking for it to be easy.

Work pleasures me no more than the next man, but if a body is to have anything there's no other way, although we found excuses enough to get up in the saddle and go perambulating around the country. Of course, that was necessary, too.

We'd chosen to locate near the opening of Deadwood Creek, with a mighty big ridge rising to the west of us, and Baldy Mountain to the east.

We had to hunt or gather for our grub, and we Sacketts were born to it. And that Nick Shadow—he might have been born in a castle, but he knew his way around with an axe, and took mighty fast to what we showed him about rustling up grub in the forest.

Working about the place and rustling for grub as we did, we kept out of sight. We didn't see anybody or even their tracks. Each of us would take a ride sometime during the day, and at night over the fire we'd tell of what we'd seen, so within a few days we were getting a fair picture of the country around.

Sometimes of a night we'd set about the fire and talk. Nick Shadow had education, but he never tired to hear our mountain expressions. We'd lost a few of them coming west, but an argument or a quarrel we still called an upscuddle, which seemed almighty funny to Nick.

"We don't have so many words as you," I told him, "so we have to make those we have stand up and do tricks. I never figured language was any stone-cold thing anyway. It's to provide meaning, to tell other folks what you have in mind, and there's no reason why if a man is short a word he can't invent one. When we speak of beans that have been shelled out of the pod we call 'em shuck-beans, because they've been shucked. It's simple, if you look at it."

"Learning," Galloway added, "isn't only schoolin'. It's looking, listening and making-do. If a man doesn't have much or if he's in wild country he'd better get himself to contemplate and contrive. Pa always taught us to set down and contemplate, take our problem and wrassel with it until there's an answer. And then we contrive. Back in the hills we couldn't buy much, and we didn't have any fancy fixin's, so we contrived. We put together what we could find and added it to something else."

Nick, he knew a powerful lot of poetry, and like most lonesome, wandering men we liked it. Sometimes of a night he'd set by the fire and recite. He knew a lot of poetry by that fellow Poe who'd died about the time I was born. He used to live over the mountain in Virginia . . . over the mountain from us, that is, who lived on the western slope of the hills.

We'd never paid much mind to Nick Shadow's talk of gold. There'd been Spanish people in Colorado from the earliest times, and for awhile there'd been French folks coming west from New Orleans when Colorado was part of the Louisiana country. The story Nick told us about the gold he knew of was known to others, too. But treasure stories come by the dozen in gold mining country, and everybody you meet has got a mine worth a million dollars or many millions, depending on how many drinks the owner's had.

One night he said, "Finding the big caches, where they hid the millions would be accident now, because nobody knows exactly where it was hidden, but there's another treasure that might be found, so I'm going to tell you about it.

"My grandfather had a brother who trapped in this country nearly fifty years ago, and much of the sign left by those early French and Spanish miners was plainly visible when he arrived in the country.

"The others had never heard the stories of the gold found in the La Platas, nor the less known stories of diamonds found there, and Arnaud was not the man to tell them of it, but he kept his eyes open, and he had an idea where to begin looking.

"No need to go into all the details, but I figure we're not more than ten miles from that gold right now."

"Ten miles is a lot of country," Galloway suggested.

"They were headed up the La Plata, planning to take an old Indian trail that follows along the ridge of the mountains, and Arnaud was counting the streams that flowed into the river. Just past what he counted as the sixth one he saw what he was looking for . . . a dim trail that led up into the peaks.

"They continued on a mile or so further and then he suggested they stop and trap out a beaver pond they'd found. Arnaud volunteered to hunt meat for them and he took off along the river, and as soon as he was out of sight of the others he started back, found his trail and started up.

"It was a steep trail, unused in a long time, and he figured that in the two miles or so of trail he climbed about three thousand feet . . . he was judging in part by the change in vegetation. He reached a high saddle, crossed over and started down. He was looking for a creek that flowed out of the mountain, and he could see the canyon down which it flowed, but there was no longer a trail. That had played out when he reached the crest of the ridge.

"It was very cold, and the going was difficult. He had to move slowly because of the altitude. He crossed over the saddle, as I've said, but he had no more than started down when he heard a shot where he had left his friends. A shot, and then several shots.

"As you can imagine, he was in a quandary. If he went back to help his friends, it would take him the better part of an hour, moving as he would have to, and by then any fight would be over.

"Or perhaps they had merely killed a deer. In the final event, he continued on, found the head of the creek and found the marker, a piece of a ramrod thrust into a crack in the rock. The gold was cached just below it and to the right, and when he removed the stones he found a dozen gold bars, several sacks of dust, and one small sack of diamonds.

"It was too much to carry and now that he knew where it was he could come back any time. He took one sack of dust and dropped a couple of the diamonds in it and thrust it into his pack. Then he recovered the gold and started back.

"There had been no more shooting, but when he came near the bottom of the hill he took great care, studying out his trail in advance. He was still some distance from the beaver pond when he saw Mohler. He was lying face down in the grass with five arrows in his back, a golden carpet of dandelions all about him.

"Arnaud watched for several minutes but there was no movement from the body, no sign of life. From where he lay he could see the dead man still had his rifle and tomahawk, so the body had not been looted.

"Easing back into the brush he worked his way

around toward the pond, and there near a fallen log he saw another one. He couldn't make out who it was, but this body had been stripped, scalped, and mutilated.

"The fact that the one body had been stripped and the other had not implied the Indians were still around, so he moved back into the brush and lay quiet, listening.

"He stayed there all day without moving on the theory that if he did not move he would make no sound and leave no tracks. Several times he saw Indians, but each time they passed some distance away, and finally they mounted up and rode away.

"When it was dark he went down to Mohler, but the man was cold in death and had been stripped and robbed in the meantime. The others, if any remained alive, were busy getting away from there, and that was what he decided to do. The Utes had gone downstream, so he went upstream with the idea of striking the high-line trail. He did, found one of the others of his party still alive, and together they got out of the country."

"But the gold is still there?"

"The gold and the diamonds. Of the two he got out with, one was worthless. The other was an excellent stone, however, and with the results he bought a small farm in French Canada."

"He never came back?"

"He decided to let well enough alone. He married, had children, but none of them were inclined toward adventure. I gathered they did not have much faith in their father's stories. Their own lives were rather prosaic and his stories were unbelievable to them . . . but not to me."

"Well," I said, "it won't do any harm to look. You say the place is close by?"

"Right back of that peak yonder. The start of that trail can't be three miles from here." He glanced over at Galloway. "Now you know why I was so willing to come along. I've been up here before, but these rivers were named when Arnaud was in here, and I wasted time on the Florida and the Animas before I realized they had to be wrong."

We brought our horses in from their picket-ropes and after watering them, turned them into the corral. Then we bedded down and went to sleep.

There for a few minutes I lay awake, considering that gold. If we had it we could buy more cattle, fix our place up better, but I wasn't counting any gold we didn't have. A lot of folks had their hands on that gold and it hadn't done any of them much good.

The fire died down to coals, and I could hear the rustling of the aspens and the faint sounds the horses made in the corral.

I wondered, suddenly, what had become of that wolf.

Chapter X

Many a campfire dies down with talk that doesn't count up to much in the sunlight.

Around the fire is the time to talk of treasure, and ha'nts and witches and such, but come broad day there's work to be done. Somewhere back down the line Parmalee Sackett should be starting north with a herd, and it was time for Nick Shadow to ride down to meet him.

It was also time for somebody to ride down to Shalako and burden themselves with grub for the next two weeks of work, and it spelled out to be me for that job. The past few days had helped a sight when it came to my strength catching up to itself, and I felt a whole lot better. Still, we didn't want to leave our place alone too long. Not that we had anything there. Galloway, he said to me, "Flagan, let's ride this out for awhile. Let's sleep out and see what they do. If there's to be a fraction over this let's not have anything they can burn." ... So we hadn't.

Nevertheless the thought of that gold was in all our minds, and it was in our thoughts to ride up there someday and have a look for it. Right now we had to pin down the things that were sure or that we were trying to make sure.

Shalako lay still under the afternoon sun when I rode into town. I was still wearing the moccasins because my feet were not quite well, and they were almighty tender around the edges where the flesh had been broken and torn and mashed by rocks, but otherwise I was dressed pretty well for the time, and for a working cowhand.

The first thing I saw was the buckboard from the Rossiter outfit, and Meg about to get down, so I swung my horse alongside and stepped down in time to take her hand and help her down.

She smiled, but I'd say it was a might cool, but when she taken my hand to step down she done it like a real lady, and I could see she set store by such things. Fact is, I set store by them myself. It pleasures a man to do graceful things for a lady, and if she's pretty, so much the better. We'd be a sorry world without the courtesies, as Ma used to say.

"My!" Meg said. "I would scarcely know you!"

Me, I blushed like a fool, which I have a way of doing whenever a woman says "I, yes, or no" to me. And the blushing makes me mad at myself, which makes me blush all the more. So I stood there, all red around the ears like a dirt-kicking country boy.

"I got me an outfit," I said finally. And then I added, "We're fixing to go ranching, me and Galloway and Nick Shadow."

"How nice!" she said primly, and then with a little edge to her voice she said, "I'm surprised you have the nerve after the way you backed down for Curly Dunn."

Now I never backed down for no man, and she knew it, but girls like to put a man in a bad place and she had done it to me. Like a fool I started in to argue the question, which I shouldn't have done. "I never backed down for him," I said, "or any man."

She turned away from me. "If I were you," she said, "I'd leave while I could. Curly is going to meet me here."

Well, now. Common sense told me that I should go, but her throwing it up to me like that . . . well, I couldn't go then. So I just turned and walked off feeling like I'd come off a pretty poor hand, but then I never was much at talking to women.

In the store I laid out to get the things we needed—flour, salt, coffee, and whatever. They had dried apples, so I laid in a stock of them, and this time I was able to pay. I'd lost whatever I had when the Indians taken me, but Galloway was carrying a good bit right then, as I had been, and whatever either one of us had the other could have. But these supplies were for all of us.

Adding to the list I bought four hundred rounds of .44-calibre ammunition.

The storekeeper, he looked up at me. "You planning a war?"

"No, sir, I ain't. But if anybody comes a-looking I wouldn't want them to go away disappointed. It ain't in my nature to leave folks a-wanting. Meanwhile we have to hunt our meat."

"The Dunns have been around. They've been talking against you."

"Talk never scratched any hides," I said. "They've got to do more than talk."

"That's what we came to town for," Curly's voice said from behind me. "I'm going to whip you right down to your socks."

"You'd have trouble," I said, "because I ain't wearing any."

And then he hit me.

He caught me as I was turning but he'd not been set proper and the punch never staggered me. I just unbuckled my gun and handed it to Berglund, who had just come in.

I think Curly was kind of surprised that I was so ready, and that I didn't get flustered and mad. So he was a mite slow with that second punch and I saw it a-coming. Now I never did want to tear up any man's store, so when that punch came at me I just ducked under it and taken him in the belly with my shoulder, wrapping one arm around his legs and rushing him right out the door.

At the edge of the porch I dropped him and he staggered so I hit him.

Now we Sackett boys grew up a-sweating with an axe, shovel, and plow. We'd worked hard all our lives and my fists were big and hard and backed by an uncommon lot of muscle, so when I fetched him a clout he went back into the middle of the street and fell down.

Stepping off the walk I walked toward him and he got up. He was big, maybe twenty pounds heavier than me, and he was in a whole lot better shape because he'd not been through what I had, but also he was a drinker, and drinking whiskey isn't what you'd call proper for a fighting man.

He came at me, a little wiser now, because that clout he'd caught had carried some power. But he wasn't worried. He'd won a lot of fights and saw no reason why he shouldn't win this one.

Me and Galloway had grown up fighting in the mountains and then we'd knocked around on riverboats and freight outfits and most of what we knew we'd learned by applying it that way.

He came in and he taken a swing at me which I pulled aside from, and when I pulled over I smashed my fist into his belly. It taken him good—right where he lived. I saw his face go kind of white and sick and then I hit him again.

He went down hard into the dust, and the next thing I know there's a crowd around yelling at him to get up. Without them I don't think he would have done it. Meg was there, too, her face all kind of white and funny, staring at him like she had never seen him before, but she didn't look scared, nor did she look altogether displeased.

What I didn't know until later was that both Ollie

Hammer and Tin-Cup were in that crowd, just a-watching.

Curly had his friends behind him and he'd made a lot of brags no doubt, so he had it to do. His first punch missed but the second caught me a rap alongside of the face and I staggered. He came on in, swinging with both hands and hit me again. We clinched and I threw him with a rolling hip-lock, and stepped back.

I was just learning how much that time in the woods had taken out of me, for I'd no staying power at all. He came at me, swinging. Again I made him miss one but caught the other one on the chin, and it hurt. So I bowed my neck and went to punching with both hands. I missed a few but some of them landed, and when they landed he gave ground.

We fought up and down in the dust for maybe three or four minutes, and then he remembered about my feet, and he stomped on my toes with his boot heel.

It hurt. It hurt me so bad I thought I'd go down, but I stayed up and seeing it had hurt, he came at me again. This time when he tried to stomp I hooked my toe under his ankle and kicked it up and around and he fell into the dust. When he did that I ran in and grabbed him by the collar and the belt, whirled him around and let go, and he hit the water trough all spraddled out.

He got up though, his face bloody and him shaken. Me, I was all in. I had to get him now or never, so I walked in and swang on him. I threw it from the hips and it caught him in the mouth and pulverized his lips. My next one split his ear and then I threw one to his belly. He pawed at me, but I had it to do now or never, and I brushed it aside and hit him with an uppercut in the belly.

His knees buckled and I went in on him, got my forearm under his chin and forced his head back, and then I swung on his belly.

Somebody grabbed me from behind and then Berglund yelled, "Lay off, Hammer! Back up now, or I'll drop you!"

He was up there on the porch with my old Dance & Park in his fist and they taken him serious.

Well, I stepped back and let Curly fall into the dust, and he just lay there, his shirt all tore up and his face bloody, as much as I could see of it.

I staggered some, and almost fell into the water trough, but splashed water on my face and chest.

When I turned around nobody in that crowd looked friendly. I could see by their faces looking like Curly that two or three of them were Dunns. "He asked for it," I said. "Now take him home."

A powerful big older man sitting a bay horse spoke up. He had a shock of hair on a big square head and he looked like he'd been carved from granite, "Boy," he said, "I'm Bull Dunn, and that's my boy. You get out of this country as fast as you can ride and maybe you'll get away. If you stay on here, I'll kill you."

"Mister Dunn," I said, "I'm staying, and you've got it to do."

He turned his eyes on me and for a moment our eyes held. I was in almighty bad shape and not wishing for any trouble with him right now. My fists were sore from the fight and I wasn't sure if I could use a gun if I had one, and I was afraid I was going to have to try.

It was Red who walked out of the saloon and leaned against a post. "Mister Dunn," he said, "you'd better give it some thought. I was with an outfit one time that tried to buck these Sackett boys and we came out at the small end of the horn."

Bull Dunn did not even seem to notice him. He merely repeated, "Get out while you can ride." Then he turned his horse and the others followed. Right there at the end Ollie Hammer turned and grinned at me, but it was not a pleasant grin. And they rode on out of town.

The storekeeper he came out on the boardwalk.

"You'd better get another hundred rounds," he said. "It does look like war."

Well, sir, I went on inside the saloon and dropped into a chair, and I was in bad shape. That fight had used me up. I was getting my strength back but I was a long way short of being the man I had been.

Berglund, he brought me a drink, and it did me good. Then he brought some coffee and he began to work on my face, patching up a couple of cuts. He had handed me back my gun when I came inside and I kept flexing my fingers, trying to get the stiffness out of them.

"You watch yourself, Sackett," he said. "They've dry-gulched more than one man."

After a long while I began to feel better, and the fresh, hot coffee helped.

They had probably been watching us, and they were sure that Nick Shadow was gone. Probably they had not guessed why he was going, but they certainly knew they had but two men to contend with, and to them that must seem like nothing at all.

Right now Galloway was up there alone, and they might choose this time to cut the odds in half. Only my brother was no pilgrim, and coming up on him unexpected was not an easy thing to do.

"I've got to get back to camp."

"You need rest," Berglund protested.

He was right, of course, but his rightness did not help. Galloway was up there alone, and while he might choose to withdraw up the mountain or up Deadwood Gulch, it was more likely that he would refuse to be pushed.

Loading supplies on a borrowed packhorse, I prepared to start back. My body was stiff and sore, and I wanted nothing so much as sleep, yet I had to get back. Even now they might be preparing an attack on Galloway, and they were a tough, mean, bitter lot.

It would be days, perhaps weeks before the others arrived, and until then we must somehow defend our

position, or at least keep it open for the arrival of
Parmalee Sackett and the return of Nick Shadow.

Mounting the *grulla* I rode into the bottom of the La
Plata, then cautiously worked my way upstream. Several times I came upon the hoofprints of horses. They
had been here then, no doubt studying what they must
do. The tracks were several days old.

Galloway was nowhere in sight when I rode up the
last few hundred yards to the corral, but he came out
of the woods, Winchester over his arm. He glanced at
my face.

"That must be quite a town," he commented, affably.
"Seems to me they hold out a welcome."

"You should try it some time. I ain't what you'd call
mincy about towns but this here one is about to try
my patience."

"Who was it?"

"Curly . . . and but for that saloonkeeper in yonder
they might have salted me away."

"You whup him?"

"I ain't sure. I feel like it was me got whupped, on'y
when it was over he lay stretched out. I bruised him. I
reckon I did."

Well, I got down and like to fell off my horse. Galloway, he taken my horse back in the woods whilst I
set by the fire, my head hanging. It was aching something awful and my mouth was cut inside, and my face
sore.

"I didn't think he had the sand," Galloway commented.

"He didn't. It was those fool friends of his, urgin'
him on. I think he wanted to quit but he was scared
of what would be said, and I was scared he wouldn't
quit before I had to fall, I was that all in."

Galloway was making soup. He got that from Ma.
Anytime anybody had anything happen, birth, death,
fight or wedding, Ma made soup.

Suddenly I saw something at the edge of the woods.

There for a moment it looked like a wolf. He was looking back the way I had come, so I turned my head to
look also.

A rider was coming up the draw. He was right out
in the open but he was coming right on, walking his
horse. He had a rifle in his hands.

Chapter XI

Even before the old man came close enough for us to make him out, I could see he was an Indian by the way he sat his horse. He came on slowly and when he drew up facing us he sat looking upon us thoughtfully.

He was the shadow of a man who had been great. I mean in a physical way. The bones were there, and the old muscles showed how once they had stretched the skin with power, and the look was there yet, in his eyes and in his carriage. He was a proud man.

"We're fixing to have some soup," I said. "Will you set up to the fire?"

He looked at me for a long minute, and then said, "Are you Sak-ut?"

The name came out short and blunt.

"We both are," I said. "We're brothers. In thinking as well as in blood. Will you get down?"

He put the rifle away and swung down. Maybe he was a mite stiff, but not enough to bother. He dropped his reins and walked to our fire with dignity. I held out my hand to him as he came up. "I am Flagan Sackett. This here is Galloway."

"Howdy," Galloway said.

He wasn't missing a thing, his eyes going from my

87

moccasins to my face. When he turned toward me again I saw there was a scar on the left side of his face from what seemed to be a powder burn.

After we had eaten, Galloway dug out the tobacco sack. Neither Galloway nor me ever taken to smoking but most Indians did and it was handy for trade. After he had puffed away for awhile he looked up and said, "I am Powder Face. I am Jicarilla."

He let that set with us for a few minutes and then he said, looking right at me, "You are warrior. I am warrior. We can talk together."

"I have heard of Powder Face," I said, "and to talk to him is an honor."

His eyes glinted, but after a few puffs at his pipe he said, "You escape from my people. You are good runner."

"I am a good fighter, too," I said, "but your folks left me without much to do with."

"You are like Indian," he said, "like Jicarilla."

Well, that was all right with me. What all this was leading up to, I didn't know, but I was willing to set and listen. Raised around the Cherokee like I was, I have some savvy for Indians and their ways, and all things considered they make out to be pretty fine folks. Their ways are different than ours, but the country was different, then.

"I come to you because you think like Indian. You fight like Indian. Maybe you will talk to Indian."

"I'll talk," I said, "and I'll listen."

"I am called renegade," he said. "My tribe is small. Some are Jicarillas, some are Tabeguache Ute. We fight, we do not surrender. Finally there are few of us, and we hide in high mountains."

He paused for a long time, but finally he said, "Our people are few. There are many Indians south or north, but we wish to fight no more. We have watched from the peaks as the white men come. A long time ago I rode far to the east, and I have seen the towns of the white man. In the north I have seen the wagon that smokes. The white man has strong medicine.

"We are twenty people. We are six warriors, seven women, and seven children. Soon there will be two more. The winter will come, and the game will come down from the peaks and we will starve.

"We do not wish to go with the Jicarillas. We do not wish to go with the Utes. There may again be war and we do not want to fight." He looked up suddenly and mighty proud. "We have been great warriors. For our lives we will fight, but we cannot leave our young ones to starve in the cold.

"You are white man. You are warrior. You are strong against pain and you know the Indian way. I come to you as to an elder brother. You will tell us what we should do."

Well, now. He was an older and no doubt a wiser man than me and he had come to me for advice. One thing I had he did not have . . . at least, not quite so much. I had knowledge of the white man. And all of what I knew wasn't good, but that was true of his people, too. We all had our good and our bad. The white man had broken treaties and the Indian had killed innocent people, and without warning. The white man had done his share of that, too.

There was no need to talk to Galloway. We two understood each other as if we were of the same mind. I didn't know what Nick Shadow might think but that we'd have to work out as best we could. I just knew what I was going to do.

"We are going to ranch here." I swept a wide gesture at the hills. "We are going to raise cattle and horses. We are going to need help. Can your young men ride?"

"Our old men can ride, too," he said proudly.

"Suppose you bring your folks down and camp over yonder." I indicated an area back against the mountain. "Your people can live here and your young men can ride for us.

"There's one more thing: your people must stay close to here at first. There are some men around who will not like it that you are here. Stay close to the ranch or in the mountains until they get used to the idea."

The old man bedded down not far from us that night, and in the morning he was gone. Galloway he looked over at me and chuckled. "You sure bought trouble," he said. "I never seen the like."

"What would you have done?"

He grinned at me. "The same thing. Only I'd not have asked him if his young men could ride. That was like askin' if a fish can swim."

"I was really asking them if they would ride," I said. "That there is what is called a rhetorical question. At least that's what Nick Shadow would call it."

"What'll he think about this?"

"He'll buy it. Nick will buy anything that's contrary to the prejudices of people around him. He's just like that. He's just naturally contrary, and he don't give a damn whether school keeps or not."

There was plenty to do before the cattle came. We scouted the range we figured to use, and we gathered wood. Usually we would just throw a loop around a log and drag it to where we could use it come snow time. There were a lot of deadfalls around, and we gathered a good many knowing a long winter was ahead and there wouldn't always be time for hunting firewood.

Then we set to notching the logs for a cabin, and we built a stoneboat for hauling stones for the fireplace. In between times one or the other of us would ride out afar from home to get an elk or a deer for meat. There were a good many beaver along the branches but we didn't figure to worry them. The pools they make back of their beaver dams help to control floodwaters and keep the water where it's needed, right on the land.

All the time we kept an eye open for that Dunn outfit, but none of them showed.

Galloway he rode down to Shalako after some extra

grub and when he came back he said, "The Dunns are bringing in a boy that Berglund was telling about. He's a youngster, about twenty-one or twenty-two, and he's hell on wheels with a rifle.

"Seems that Red was in and dropped us the word, to be passed on by Berglund. This youngster is a dead shot and he's the kind that lays up in the country and watches for a good shot. He says the Dunns came into this country from a real mean fight, and this kid done half their killing for them. His name is Vern Huddy."

Now there's no safe way when a sharpshooter is coming against you. He's only got to find himself a place and wait until he gets his shot and he usually needs only one. First off, all you can do is try to keep him from getting that one shot. Don't set yourself up for him, don't skyline yourself or stand still out in the open, and when you ride, keep your eyes open and watch your horse. He'll usually know before you do if anybody is around. Always keep a good background for yourself, something that swallows you up, sort of.

However, we taken to scouting the country. We'd been doing that, but now we were even more careful. We skirted our area about a hundred yards around, checking for tracks, then a circle about three hundred yards out, and then out to a quarter of a mile.

And then I saw the wolf.

I had killed a deer and cut it up to take back to camp, when I saw that wolf, so I taken a piece of the fresh meat and tossed it to him. He disappeared, but a moment later when I glanced back the meat was gone.

There was something peculiar about that wolf. Why had he left the others and taken to following me? Did I have the smell of death on me?

When I was almost back to camp I happened to turn in my saddle and caught just a glimpse of the wolf as he dodged into the brush, so I fished another chunk of meat from the hide where I carried it and dropped it into the road. Why I did so I've no idea. Maybe I figured it was better deer meat than me meat.

Galloway had moved our camp about a hundred yards back into the brush. He was making sourdough bread when I came in and he had a pot of beans setting in the outer coals. "I don't like it, Flagan. Our boys should be showing up by now. I don't like it a-tall."

"Come daylight I'll cut across the hills. I'll study the trail."

"You ride wary. Trouble's shaping up. I can feel it in my bones."

The sun wasn't up when I mounted the *grulla* and taken to the hills. The old Dance & Park six-shooter was shoved down in its scabbard, but I carried my Winchester in my hands. It was not yet light, so I rode right back into the trees, riding up through the timber until I struck an old bear walk.

This was no regular trail, but even so I didn't hold to it long, suddenly starting up the hill on an angle, and so it was that I glimpsed something down below in the brush. It was that wolf, and he was keeping ahead of me.

Of a sudden he brought up short. He lifted one foot, then ducked into the brush like a shot.

My feet kicked free of the stirrups and I went off that horse like I'd been shot, and I almost was. As my feet hit dirt I heard the boom of a shot and I threw myself forward in the brush, then scrambled up and ran in a short dash to where an outcropping thrust up from the mountain. I was just in time to see a man legging it for his horse and I could see the horse, so I threw up my rifle and shot at the tree it was tied to. I made a wild guess as to where the reins would be tied, and either cut one or the horse broke it with his lunge when fragments of bark stung its face. Anyway the horse broke loose and when the man lunged into view again I put a bullet where he should have been but he dove into the brush.

FLINT
IF HE HAD TO DIE, AT LEAST IT WOULD BE ON HIS TERMS...

Get a taste of the *true* West, beginning with the tale of *FLINT* FREE for 15 Days

Hunted by a relentless hired gun in the lava fields of New Mexico, Flint "*settled down to a duel of wits that might last for weeks...Surprisingly, he found himself filled with zest for the coming trial...So began the strange duel that was to end in the death of one man, perhaps two.*"

If gripping frontier adventures capture your imagination, welcome to The Louis L'Amour Collection! It's a handsome, hardcover series of thrilling sagas by the world's foremost Western authority and author.

Each novel in The Collection is a true-to-life portrait of the Old West, depicted with gritty realism and striking detail. Each is enduringly bound in rich, Sierra-brown leatherette, with padded covers and gold-embossed titles. And each may be examined and enjoyed for 15 days. FREE. You are never under any obligation; so mail the card at right today.

Now in handsome Heritage Editions

Each matching 6" x 9" volume in The Collection is bound in rich Sierra-brown leatherette, with padded covers and embossed gold title... creating an enduring family library of distinction.

Taking a running jump I hit the saddle as the mustang took off and we went down that slope just a hellin'. Another shot cut close to me and I let drive with two, firing my rifle off my hip into the brush and when that mustang hit the brush it went right on through. Out in the open beyond a man was legging it down the slope. He stopped, whirled around and came up with a rifle, and I let go at him again and he spun around and dropped.

When I came up on him he was sitting there, holding his side, an ugly look in his eyes. "You played hell," he said. "They'll kill you for this."

"That's what you tried to do to me," I replied "Are you Vern Huddy?"

"Me? No, I ain't. Lucky for you, I ain't. He ain't here yet. If I'd been Vern Huddy you'd be dead. I'm Jobe Dunn, if you want to know, cousin to Curly."

His rifle dropped when my bullet hit him, but he was still wearing a six-shooter. Either he'd forgotten it or he was hoping I had. "Take it out," I said, "with two fingers. Throw it just as far out as you can. And don't try anything funny unless you want to feed the buzzards right from where you're at."

He drew that pistol and dropped it, and I swung down and gathered up his pistol and his rifle.

"Now you get on your feet and start for home, and don't stop this side of there."

"Hell, that's a good eight miles."

"It must be," I agreed. "Make a nice walk for you. Better not pass out along the way or you might die before somebody gets to you."

"You just ain't a kindly man," he protested.

"Nope. No more kindly than I'd be if I was lyin' up there on that slope dead from your bullet. I guess you figured you'd kill me your ownself and then go back and brag how you'd done it. How you'd beaten Vern to the punch."

"Vern? You're crazy! I wouldn't cross Vern for all the

tea in China. He's meaner than you are, and a whole sight better with a gun."

"Maybe."

When he set off a-walking I went back up through the trees and found my trail.

And it surely wasn't intentional that when nightfall was coming on I saw the lights of the Rossiter place. Took me all of a minute to decide to ride down there and share potluck with them. There was a chance that I'd run into Curly, but a good chance that I'd not, and a few good home-cooked vittles wouldn't go at all bad . . . or seeing Miss Meg, either.

However, before I decided to settle in for the night I'd just make sure Curly wasn't there. No use stirring up trouble on their doorstep. It was bad enough that I had shooting to think of without worrying them.

Rossiter was just unsaddling a gray gelding when I came into the yard. "How are you, boy? Light an' set."

"Don't mind if I do, only there's been shooting trouble and there'll be more, so I'd better ask. Are you expecting Curly Dunn?"

"No."

"All right then. I'll stop and gladly."

"Now just a minute. I said I wasn't expecting him, and I am not, but that doesn't mean he might not show up. He's coming over here every few days."

Nevertheless, the warmth and comfort of a woman-kept house was too much for me to turn down, so I stripped the gear from the mustang and turned it into the corral.

We walked side by each up to the house and he spoke of the shooting trouble. "I knew there were hard feelings, but I didn't know it had come to that." So I told him about Jobe taking a shot at me.

"Was he hurt bad?"

"I didn't examine him. Looked to me like a burn along the ribs, and he may lose a good deal of blood.

Maybe I nicked the inside of his arm, too. He was holding it mighty odd."

We went in the door and Meg was there and she said, "Pa, supper's ready. Who're you talking to?" And then she seen me.

"Oh . . . *you?*" she said disdainfully. "I was hoping it was Curly."

"If he's got over his beating," I said, "I'll bet he wasn't able to kiss you for a week, with those mashed-up lips of his."

"That's probably why you hit him there," she accused.

"Are you funnin'? I never gave it no thought. Why should I care who he kisses? Anyway, we weren't fighting over you. We were fighting because he had an awfully big opinion of himself and he figured to teach me something."

"I don't care why you fought," she said irritably. "You were like two animals! Now sit down and eat."

So I sat down. And she could really fix grub. I told her so. "Ma'am, for a woman with a harpy's tongue you can surely put vittles together. I declare, it's a wonder some man hasn't sweet-talked you into marrying him."

"I've never heard any sweet-talk from you!"

"No, ma'am, I was never given to it. I reckon I'd just have to bundle a girl up in my arms and kiss her real good. I wouldn't be much for talking."

"Why pick her up?" she demanded. "That's no way to do."

"Well, now. If she was as short as you—"

She stepped right up to me. "I'm not all that short!"

"Maighdlin!" Rossiter said sharply. "Put the supper on the table."

She finished putting supper on the table and she had no more to say all through it, but while Rossiter and me talked of cattle and beef prices and how a herd might increase, I kept a-thinking that maybe she wasn't that short. Especially if she stood on tiptoe.

Chapter XII

It didn't do me any good to stall around the next morning, although I never taken so long to saddle a horse in all my born days. Nor so long over breakfast, either. I was hoping Meg would show up but she didn't and after awhile I swung into the saddle and rode off up the trail.

When I was maybe a mile off and away higher up I glanced back in time to see a small figure come running from the ranch house and stop there in the yard, and I lifted my arm and waved, but surely she could not see me at the distance and against the mountain.

Two days of riding it needed before I came up with the herd. I saw their dust long before I rode up to it, but when I came near I swung off to one side so's not to turn them. Whoever was riding point had gone off somewhere, but that big old brindle steer in the lead needed no help.

Halfway down the herd I came up to Parmalee, looking like a dude. He pulled in and thrust out his hand, and dude he might be but he had power in that grip. I had a feeling those flatland Sacketts had much to be said for them other than money, for they were all well off. Nick Shadow rode up from the drag and allowed he was glad to see me. It had been a hard drive.

"You're coming into good range now," I said, "but nothing like what your headed for along the La Plata."

"We'll need some hands," Parmalee said. "Most of these just joined up for the drive."

"You got anything against Indians?"

"No . . . why?"

"I've just taken on a whole set of them. Tough old warrior and some followers of his. He came to me hunting advice, and looking for a place to light."

"So you took them on," Shadow said. "Good for you."

He looked at my face, which still carried a few scars. "You've had trouble, then?"

"I had a difficulty with Curly Dunn. I was in no shape for it, but I whopped him. A couple of days back I had a run in with Jobe. I scratched him with a bullet, but don't take them lightly, old Bull Dunn is a tough man."

"Old?"

"Aw, you know! He ain't that old. Maybe forty, but he must weight about two hundred and fifty pounds and I don't think any of it is fat."

We rode along together, the three of us, talking things over and reminding ourselves of other days, other cattle, other drives. Time to time I kept looking back into my mind for pictures of Meg, knowing I was a damned fool all the time I was doing it. She was like every other girl that age who likes to flirt and think about love and such. Curly had the inside track there, and I knew it, but that couldn't keep a body from dreaming, and dreamable girls were almighty scarce in this country.

It was on that drive that I learned that Shadow was one of the best hands with a rope I'd ever come across. He used the rawhide rope, the *la reata* that Americans have cut down to lariat. He'd learned it from the Californios, and he worked with a rope sixty feet long. He could really make that rope stand up and perform. He never tied fast, though. A man who ties fast with a rawhide rope is in trouble. When a big steer, say a thousand pounds give or take a few, hits the end of that rope something's got to give. A hemp rope will stand the gaff better, but Shadow liked rawhide and he stuck with it, and I never saw anybody who could rope any better.

He was a good hand with stock and he never shied from doing his fair share of the work. They had brought eighteen hundred head of mixed stuff, and a few of them were Texas longhorns, big, rangy beasts who could walk the legs off any other kind of cow crittur and most horses. They'd brought the herd along carefully and they didn't seem to have lost much weight on the trail.

Aside from Parmalee and Shadow there were just four hands and the cook, which was nowhere near enough even after the herd was trail broke. Seven hands were all right as long as there was no trouble. Now that I had come along there were eight and that extra man meant all the difference.

"I can't figure it," I said that night at the fire. "Bull Dunn told everybody he was going to run us out. He's made his brags, now he's got to make good, so why hasn't he done something?"

"Maybe he was waiting until Galloway was alone," Parmalee suggested.

"He's waiting for the cattle," Shadow said. "What does he gain by running you out? He keeps the country to himself, but is that enough? If he runs you out after you have your cattle brought in then those cattle are going to run loose on the range, and after a respectable time he'll just start slapping his brand on them all. And who's to stop him?"

"If that's the case," Parmalee suggested, "he'll stampede our cattle as soon as we're close to his range . . . or sooner."

Morning came bright and clear, and the cattle started off well. Maybe it was the smell of fresh water, maybe it was the grass, but the cattle wanted to go. We had the towering wall of Mesa Verde on the east and Ute Park on the west, and soon we would start bearing east to strike the trail to the ranch.

Suddenly one of the cowhands rode up. "Sackett," he said, "we're being watched." He pointed toward the distant ridge. "Indians!"

Sure enough, there were several Indians watching us from the ridge, and as we moved along they kept pace with us, watching our every move.

The Dunn ranch house was long, low and built of logs. Cornered against it and forming a right angle was the bunkhouse, where there were bunks for twenty men, and thirty yards away, forming another side to the loose square, was a barn or shed, also low-roofed and built of logs. The fourth side of the square was the corral.

Inside the house, seated at the table, was Bull Dunn. A huge man with bulging muscles, he slouched at the table with a pot of black coffee and a jug of whiskey, staring at Curly with narrowed eyes.

"You listen, and you listen damn well," he said—then his eyes swept the room—"and this goes for you all. I seen countries change. I ain't so young as you, and I seen them grow up. Well, when they do those folks who hold land are the ones in power, they run things. Those who don't have nothin' are shoved out.

"This here's the end of it. We're going to latch onto a big chunk of this country and we're going to hold it. We're through bein' movers. Here's where we make our stand.

"The Sacketts are bringing in a herd. That's fine, because we'll need stock. There's two of them and this Nick Shadow. I happen to know the cowhands comin' in with the herd won't stay. Anyway, there's only four of them.

"We're goin' to hit that herd of a night, and we're goin' to scatter it to hell an' gone into the breaks of the canyons, and we're going to kill the Sacketts and Shadow. If one of them goes down from a fall or is hurt in the stampede, just leave him lay. We want this to look as right as it can be . . . not that there's much chance of anybody nosin' around up here.

"Curly, you been sparkin' that Rossiter gal long enough. Marry her, with old Rossiter's let-be or not. You latch onto her, then you be the nice lad and you go over there and work for her papa, and you work hard. I want Rossiter to tell folks what an all-out fine son-in-law he's got. Then if anything happens to Rossiter nobody will ever think you had a hand in it.

"Then I want ever' last one of you to file on claims, grazing land or minging claims, just so you claim title to it.

"We been wanderin' around the country long enough, and the land is fillin' up back east and we might as well have ours while we can. This is closed-off country, and if we move right it'll be our country and sooner or later we can freeze out anybody who moves in."

Ollie Hammer rolled a cigarette, touched the paper with his tongue and folded it over. "Maybe you're cuttin' a wide swath, Bull. These Sacketts have the name of bein' rough."

"So are we. On'y we're rougher and meaner. I got Vern comin' in and when he gets here he'll take to the hills and clean up anything we left over. . . . As for the stampede, we blame it on the Utes."

He downed his whiskey and refilled the glass to the halfway mark, then took a gulp of the black coffee.

"We done this before, and you all know what to do. I want nobody *seen*. And get this into your thick heads. We ain't outlaws no more . . . we ain't renygades . . . so when you go into Shalako or any other town, you act like gents. If you can't hold your liquor, don't drink.

"Get this—" Bull Dunn pointed with a stiff middle finger, "some folks are goin' to complain . . . let 'em.

But if we mind our p's an' q's we'll end up with a good many folks on our side.

"Now they can't have more than three men on the night ridin' job, and three ain't goin' to stop any herd of near two thousand head. If we can stampede those cattle right over their camp, so much the better . . . we might just take out a Sackett in the process.

"But remember this. I want nobody *seen!* An' Curly, as soon as ever this is over, you ride hell bent for election back here, get you a fresh horse and go on over to Rossiters' place. Tell 'em your horse spooked a couple of times, and you think there's Indians about. Rossiter will likely get up, but you offer to set up with a rifle.

"Above all, if one of them Sacketts should show up over there, you be friendly. You put yourself out to do it. And you act the gent, see?"

When all had scattered, Bull Dunn drained his glass, gulped another cup of black coffee, then stretched out on his bed. He was not worried. His outfit had scattered or rustled herds across seven states in the past dozen years and nobody had ever caught up with them yet. Of course, there was a lot of places where they could not return, but they had no idea of going back, anyway.

This place he liked, and here he was going to stay. He chuckled in his beard. More than one old-time cattleman had rustled a few head and then put on the coat of respectability, and so could he . . . and he would enjoy it, chuckling all the time at how he had fooled them.

Curly worried him. Rossiter was too shrewd a man to fool, so as soon as ever Curly was married up with that Rossiter girl, they'd have to do something about Rossiter. In this rough country with half-wild horses and cattle, with dangerous trails and rough winters, a lot of people disappeared.

He was tired of moving, and this was the best country he had found. Right here he would stay.

The Sacketts' herd moved north and then turned
east. In the mountains, their horses grazing nearby,
the Dunns played cards, slept, or talked in a desultory
fashion as they waited.

Galloway Sackett saddled a horse to ride into
Shalako. With a trail herd coming there'd be more
hands to be fed, and they would need more grub.

Far to the east, at a stage stop not far from Pagosa
Springs, a big man on a sorrel horse rode up to the
hitch rail and dismounted. The hostler, his team ready
for the incoming stage, glanced at the horse.

"That's a mighty fine animal, but you're riding it
hard."

"I got a ways to go." The big man with the shaggy
hair had a bullet hole through his flat-brimmed hat,
and he wore a low-slung gun, tied down. "You got a
horse you want to swap? I'd want as good a horse as
I'm trading."

"Only one around is a strawberry roan over in the
stable. I don't know if the owner would swap or not.
But he might sell. He's in a poker game and he's losing
ground fast."

The big stranger walked across the hard-packed yard.
He wore a beat-up sheepskin coat and striped pants.
His boot heels were run down. He walked into the
stable, glanced at the horse, then untied the knot and
took it outside where he walked it around a good bit.
When he retied the horse he walked back. He took the
stub of a cigar from his pocket and put it between his
teeth. He lighted up, then squinted over it at the hostler.
"That man in there? He's surely losin'?"

"He was unless it's changed in the last five minutes.
Mister, you'd not go wrong on that horse. It can run
and it can stay."

"I figured it. Will you hold mine for me? I'll be
comin' back through in a few days. I got me a little
business to tidy up . . . family business."

The big stranger walked into the stage station. In
one corner of the room near the ticket window three

people were sitting, concerned with their own affairs, luggage on the floor beside them. At the other end of the room was a bar and there were several tables. A poker game was going on at one of them.

The big man walked to the bar and ordered a beer, and taking it in his hand, strolled over to where the game was being played. The owner of the horse was immediately obvious.

His brow was beaded with sweat and he was peering at the cards he held close to his chest. Two of the players had dropped out of the hand, and the two remaining were obviously card sharps. The big man knew both of them by sight but it was none of his affair. A man who played poker should not play unless he could pay, and if he played with a pair of card mechanics it was his tough luck.

The man with the diamond scarf pin tossed two chips into the pot. "Up twenty," he said. The other card sharp did likewise.

"Now wait just a minute," the loser said. "I'll raise the money. I'll—"

"I'll let you have twenty for your horse," the gambler with the scarf pin suggested.

"And I'll give him thirty-five," the big stranger said. "Cash on the barrelhead."

The gambler looked up his eyes level. "You were not invited into this discussion," he said pointedly. "Mr. Liggitt and I were discussing a business deal."

"And I put in my bid," the stranger said, and he was not smiling.

"Look here!" Liggitt objected. "That's a fine horse! That horse is worth a lot of money!"

"He's worth what I say he is worth," the gambler replied harshly. "And you've got just two minutes. Put up, or shut up."

"My offer at thirty-five stands," the big stranger said.

The gambler's gaze was deadly. "I am getting a bit tired of you," he said. "Just a little tired."

"Wait a minute!" Liggitt said. "I'll take that bid! Thirty-five it is."

The gambler's eyes remained on the big man's. "I told you," he said evenly, "that I was—"

The gambler was not really a gambler. He was a man who played with marked cards and loaded dice, and when he used a gun he did not gamble either. Suddenly a little warning bell was ringing in his ears. This big man was too confident, too ready . . . and he wasn't worried. Not the least bit.

"Give him the thirty-five," the gambler said, "and let's get on with the game."

The big man thrust his hand into his pocket and the gambler went for his gun. By ordinary standards he made a good try. The only visible gun on the big man was in a holster on his leg, his right hand was in his pocket.

The stranger drew and fired . . . drew a gun from his waistband with his left hand and shot the gambler through the third button of his vest.

There was a moment of silence and the acrid smell of gunsmoke. Liggitt slowly pulled back from the table, his face a sickly white. "I'll be goin'," he said. "I guess I'll be goin'."

"Wait." The big man put thirty-five dollars on the table. "A bill of sale for one strawberry roan with a white stocking and a Rafter Open A brand."

"The game's over. There's no need for me to sell."

"You agreed. You taken my offer." The big man looked around. "I leave it to you all. He taken my offer, didn't he?"

It was unanimous. Liggitt looked around, sweating. Reluctantly he made out the bill of sale and picked up the thirty-five dollars.

"That horse is worth a lot more," he protested.

"That he is," the big man agreed, "so I suggest that as long as the game is over, and nobody knows how it would have turned out, you take half of what's on the table."

The other gambler recovered his voice. "Like hell!" he said. "I won this fair and square! I—"

The big man's smile was not pleasant "My friend," he said, "my advice is to let well enough alone. If you get half of this it will give you a roadstake, and that's more than you're entitled to. Now don't make me start reading from the Book. You ain't even very good at what you've been doin', so let it ride."

The gambler sat back carefully. "All right," he said to Liggitt, "fifty-fifty."

The hostler had come in and was standing near the door. "I put your saddle on the roan. I'll hold your horse for you until you come back."

"Thanks."

The big man watched while Liggitt and the other gambler split what was on the table, then he turned and went out, his spurs tinkling softly as he walked.

There was a silence when he left, then the gambler sighed. He looked over at the hostler. "Did you know that man?"

"No, sir, but I seen him before. I seen him a couple of times. That was Logan Sackett."

The gambler looked at his hands, they were trembling. Then he glanced at the body of his partner. "You damned fool!" he said softly. "You poor damned fool!"

The sound of hoofs pounded away into silence, and the bartender came around from behind the bar. "Jim," he said to the hostler, "you take his heels."

Chapter XIII

The weather turned off hot, and riding to the windward of that herd was plain murder with the heat coming off their bodies in a wave. Nobody wanted it much or long, and me no more than the others.

Me or Shadow held to the point a good part of the time for we alone knew the trail. It was work. The cattle had turned ornery with the heat and just plain didn't wish to travel, nor to be guided when they did travel.

They seen the mountains yonder and wanted to hole up in some of those shady canyons close upon a running stream, and I felt as they did, but necessity demanded we march along.

The Indians who had followed us along the Mesa Verde cliffs disappeared. Maybe they'd come to a place where it was no longer possible, and maybe they had something else in mind. I hoped they weren't figuring on a scrap. It was too blamed hot.

The way ahead was narrowing down some and beyond there it widened out with a lot of broken country to north and south, and the Mancos River ahead. Pulling up I let the herd roll by and waited for Parmalee to come up.

First time I ever saw him look dusty. But only a

mite. He reined in and we let them go by, and he said,
"We'll water this side of the Mancos? Didn't you say
there was a creek?"

"If there's water in it."

"If not, then the Mancos."

Parmalee had his rifle in his hand, and he pointed
with it. There were Indians coming, right down the
slope from Mesa Verde, but this was no raiding party.
There were only seven . . . no, eight of them.

It was Powder Face.

"Hold it," I said to Parmalee, "these are the Indians
I hired."

Powder Face stopped and the others gathered
around him. Two of them were mere boys, not over
fourteen. "We come work if you see proper."

I started to welcome them and then had a hunch.
"Powder Face," I said, "you can do us more good if you
hold off until night.

"I think," I added, "somebody is going to try to
stampede our cattle, and steal them. Once everybody is
in camp, three men will be on guard, then when the
night is half gone they will sleep, and three more
will ride. I want you to hide out, then move in at night
and help guard the herd.

"This herd," I added, "is your winter meat as well
as ours, and it is meat for many seasons. If the cattle
are driven off, I cannot feed you."

"We watch," he said. "You ride."

Like smoke they were gone, leaving nothing but a
scattering of tracks. To anybody who watched it would
have seemed they had tried to beg beef and we had
turned them away.

We bedded the herd down on a little branch about
five miles west of the Mancos, with good grass all
around. They grazed for awhile, then lay down. Parmalee, Munson, and the two Tyler boys taken the first
night-herd, with me, Nick Shadow and Charlie Farnum,
a breed, taking the second.

It was one of those still, beautiful nights when a body

could hear a stick break a half-mile away. I didn't hear anything. I was dog-tired and wanting a bath and so hungry I couldn't finish my grub. I just went and crawled under my soogan and was asleep in no time.

Parmalee woke me up at one o'clock. "We stood it another hour," he said, "as it was quiet. The wind's coming up, so be careful."

Tugging on my boots I said, "See anything of those Injuns?"

"We won't, will we?"

"Prob'ly not. They're probably off in the woods fast asleep." But I was joking and Parm knew it. Those Indians were out there, and they were hearing and seeing everything.

Squatting by the fire I tried to blink the sleep from my eyes while pouring a cup of coffee. It was hot, and black as the hinges of hell, but it tasted good. I picked up a chunk of sourdough bread and some jerky and chewed on it while waiting for Shadow.

He was a sullen man on being awakened in the night and wanted to talk to nobody. In the night I always felt good and took to awakening at any hour with no problems. I also could do a fair job of sleeping at any hour, given the chance, which was rare.

Charlie Farnum never talked much at any time so he and Nick were suited. And I had sense enough to keep my trap shut. We all sat around the fire staring at it with blank faces like so many bumps on a log, slowly letting the coffee take the kinks out of us. After awhile I got up and went out to throw my kak on a little buckskin I was using for a night horse.

It could move like a cat and see like one, and was a horse I trusted for night work, and she seemed to take to me. It nuzzled at me and I fed it a chunk of carrot I had swiped from the chuckbox.

In the western lands a man had best be good friends with his horse or he may never have another friend or need of one. A man afoot in wild country is a man who may not live out the day . . . which is why horse-

stealing was the major sin. In many cases if you stole
a man's horse you condemned him to death, a much
less pleasant death than if you'd just up and shot him.

The buckskin humped its back a couple of times to
show me it was in good shape and ready for work and
also that it would take no nonsense from its rider. That
horse wanted to know I was wide awake, and after
those bumps she gave me, I was.

Shadow and Farnum followed and we rode out,
checking in with the riders we relieved and saw them
drift off to the fire. They'd probably have coffee, chew
the fat a little and then hit the sack, for they were a
tired lot. Cattle drives don't leave a man much in the
spirit of playing the night owl. There's nothing like a
long cattle drive for making a good Christian out of a
man . . . for at least as long as the drive lasts.

That little buckskin taken out, moving around the
herd. Things look different at night, so on the first couple
of trips around I was mostly locating landmarks and
spotting the known troublemakers among the steers.
This being a mixed herd it was more apt to stampede
then had it been one or the other, but we had a
couple of steers and one cow that were plumb flighty,
ready to jump at the slightest noise.

We sang to 'em. Then they hear your voice coming
and aren't startled by you. Ride up quick on a steer
and he's liable to jump right off the ground and run
clean out of the county. My voice isn't much, but I
often used to tell folks I was a singer, and that I'd sung
for crowds of up to three thousand. I didn't tell them
I was talking of cows, but they had heard my voice
and probably guessed. Galloway might have made 'em
believe it, he was that much of a singer.

Shadow stopped to talk when we met the second
time around. "The breed was telling me he thinks its
too quiet. Nothing stirring out in the brush, and there
should be."

"Well, let's play it that way," I said. "Let's stay on
our toes."

"What do you think about it?"

"Look," I said, "if something starts them running we got to keep them off the boys so they won't get tramped. Let's make it so each time we pass the camp we slow up so there's somebody in position most of the time. Then if the cattle start to run, try to keep them headed east and out of the canyons. If they get into those canyons and up into the breaks we'll never get them out before snow flies, and that means we'll never get them out."

It was still over an hour before daylight when all of a sudden somebody stepped out of the trees and stood there. Rifle ready, I rode up, although waiting for me like that he wasn't apt to be an enemy. It was an Indian.

"Powder Face say tell you man come . . . maybe ten, twelve man."

"Thanks," I said, but the Indian did not fade into the brush.

"Powder Face say he thinks they try Indian trick. Use mountain-lion skin."

And that time he did disappear, but it was a comfort to know they were close by.

Nick Shadow closed in. "Was that you talking?"

So I told him. He knew the trick as well as me. The Indians used to do it with a fresh puma hide. They'd get in close and wave the skin and the cattle would get that smell of cat, and then one of the Indians would imitate the scream and those cattle would be gone.

We started on and I was almost to the camp when I heard that scream, and those cattle came off the ground with a lunge. They made a break toward the camp and I jerked out my pistol and let go with a shot into the air and a wild, Comanche yell. Some of them veered, but some of the others I couldn't reach and they went through camp just a hellin'. Pots and pans went every which way. I heard a pistol shot and then another and then a scream, and all of a sudden that herd was gone.

All that was left was dust and the sound of thundering hoofs.

They were headed for the Mancos River and that was one of the reasons I'd stopped where I had. If they had a run of several miles and then reached the river they might stop to drink. This bunch was pretty fat anyway, and they weren't like a bunch of wild longhorns all hungry for water who might run for hours.

Wheeling around I rode into camp. It was a shambles. First off I saw a man on the ground or what had been a man. It was one of the Tyler boys. The only way I could tell was by the silver conchas he wore on his belt.

Even as I swung up, Parmalee came down out of a tree. The cook came out of the rocks, and the other two had taken shelter behind the wagon. My pistol shot had come just in time to give them a split second.

"Tyler," I said, "you and Cookie take care of him." I indicated the dead man. "Parm, you'd best go help with your cattle."

"What about you?" he asked.

"I'm going to ride up the canyon. I want to read some sign."

"I'll go with you."

"No. I'll take Charlie Farnum. Unless I'm mistaken you'll find your herd at the river and my Indians will be there too."

Nick Shadow had gone down after the cattle, but I'd heard Farnum's horse slow down and I figured he had the same idea I had. I rode out from the camp and he was a-settin' there waiting for me.

"Figured you might like to look around," he said, and we started walking our horses slow, keeping to the open ground where we made less sound. Once we drew up to listen, and after a moment Charlie said, "Why you do that for those Indians?"

"They're good folks," I said, "and this was their country. It's nobody's fault as to what's happened.

Wherever there's open country there'll be people coming hungry for land, and it wouldn't have made much sense to let a lot of folks in Europe starve to death when there was miles and miles of unused land awaiting.

"The Indian would have had a better deal, and should have but for a lot of greedy white men and because of a few scalp-hungry Indians. There was right and wrong on both sides. I'm doing no crying for the Indian. He made his fight but he never could get enough guns and ammunition and the white men kept moving in, but when old Powder Face came to me he came honest, and he told me who he was and what he'd done, and I made him welcome. I figure those boys will make good hands and as far as I'm concerned they're here forever."

After that we shut up and rode on, and pretty soon we noticed our horses ears go up like they saw something or smelled something, and sure enough there was a fire, and a half dozen men around it, and one young feller had that cat hide in his hands and he was laughing at the way the herd took off. The rest of them must have been off following the herd. I figured Powder Face and Nick Shadow would take care of them.

"Charlie," I said, "you shoot the first one that moves."

When I spoke I spoke loud and you never saw a bunch of men come to stillness any swifter. Then I stepped down there and I looked at the tall blond ranny with the hide in his hands and I said, "You killed a good man tonight, a better man than you'll ever be. So you drop that hide and go for your gun."

"Can I put the hide down first?"

"Any way you like," I said, "but have at it."

Me, I was mad clear through. They'd tried to wipe out our camp and kill us all. It was pure-dee luck that they hadn't done it.

"You're a Sackett," this tall ranny said. "Well, Sackett, I'm Abel Dunn, and I'm going to save Rocker his job."

He let go the hide and his hand swept down and closed over that six-shooter and my gun stabbed flame at him twice, so close together they looked and sounded like one. And he folded and went down.

"That's for Tyler," I said. "Now old Bull Dunn warned me out of the country. You take Abel back to him wrapped in that cougar hide, and you tell Bull Dunn he can leave the country or stay, it don't make me no mind, but if he stays he better start goin' to Sunday School and actin' like it."

"You talk big," one of them said. "Wait until Rocker hears about this."

"You tell him," I said. "You just ride fast and tell him."

"You're the one better leave. You got no more herd than nothing."

"You wasted your time," I said. "My herd's down at the Mancos right now, and its all in one piece and my boys are with it. You started your victory party a mite too soon."

I could see several bottles around camp so I put bullets in them, and when one of them thinking my gun was empty started to reach, Charlie Farnum put a bullet through his arm.

Right there in front of them I shoved the shells out of that old Dance & Park pistol and loaded up again. And then I went in there and emptied their guns, dropping the shells into the fire and throwing their guns into the brush. Then I taken off.

In about a minute shells began to pop and those Dunn people scrambled for shelter.

Charlie Farnum and me we started east for the herd, riding together. When we were a few miles off we started to sing, and we sang a dozen songs before we shut up and left it to the coyotes.

That Charlie Farnum had a better voice than me.

For that matter, so did the coyotes.

Chapter XIV

On the second morning after the stampede, and knowing nothing whatever about it, Galloway Sackett headed for town.

He chose a new route, avoiding the trail they had used, and crossing the La Plata well above Shalako. He stayed in the trees and brush, keeping out of sight until close to town, then he emerged from the woods behind the livery stable and rode around in front of Berglund's place.

Crossing the street to the store he swung down and tied his horses. Inside he ordered rice, beans, flour, and whatever it seemed likely they would need. He sacked it up and loaded it on the packhorse.

The town was empty and still. Occasionally the music box from the saloon would brighten the day with tin-panny music. In the distance there was snow on the mountains. Galloway paused in tying his pack and stared at it, thinking he'd like to go up there. He'd never been that high up in the mountains. It was then he remembered Nick Shadow's story about the gold and diamonds.

He glanced thoughtfully toward the peaks. Now if he could just take a little trip up there . . .

The rope came snaking from the shadows beside the

store and the loop dropped over his head, pinning his
arms to his sides. He swore at himself for daydreaming
at such a time and made a desperate attempt to reach
his gun. A jerk from the rope sprawled him on the
boardwalk, and then another loop fell over his legs.
He heard a laugh boom out and another rider rode
out from behind the store leading three horses.

He started to speak and they jerked him into the
dust, dragging him a few feet. Then one of them walked
over and drew Galloway's gun from its scabbard and
thrust it behind his own waistband.

Curly Dunn still wore the fading blue marks left
from the bruises Flagan had given him, and there was
a scarcely healed cut over his eye.

"We got us a Sackett, boys. Let's take him over into
the tree and give him the Injun treatment."

Arms and legs held tight by the nooses, there was
not a thing he could do. If he made a move they would
jerk him and drag him, so he waited. Inwardly, he
was desperate.

Flagan was miles away with Nick Shadow and Parmalee. He could expect no help from the townspeople
who were trying to stay out of the trouble, and for
which he did not blame them. They could do nothing
against the Dunns, who could simply burn them out
and ride on. Nor had he any reason to believe they
even knew of his situation. In any event the total pop-
ulation of Shalako at this moment numbered just five
people.

There was nobody to help him. He must not struggle,
but must bide his time, hoping to catch them off guard.
If he struggled they would only jerk the ropes tighter,
making escape more difficult.

Curly swung his horse and started for the trees, the
others following. Suddenly one of them pulled up.

"Curly, we should ought to have us a bottle. This
here may take some time, and his sweatin' may make
us thirsty."

"All right, go get it then. You got money?"

"I have," the other one broke in.

"You two go an' get the liquor, but hurry back. You don't want to miss the fun. Alf, you loosen that rope around his legs. I want him to walk to it."

Galloway made no move as Alf loosened the ropes. The two turned then and went toward the saloon. Curly grinned at Galloway. "Here's where I get a little of my own back. We're goin' to see how loud a Sackett can yell."

"You'll wait a long time," Galloway said quietly.

Curly laughed and started for the trees. Galloway had to trot to keep up. Once he fell and Curly dragged him several yards before he stopped and allowed him to rise. And then just as he was on his feet, Curly jerked him sharply so that he hit the ground hard. Curly laughed. "How's it feel, Sackett? That ain't nothin' to what's comin'. How do your toes stand up to fire? Pa tried that on a Yankee one time who wouldn't tell us where he'd hidden his proud-ofs. He told us soon enough, but pa let the fire burn for awhile just to teach him a lesson."

They were well into the trees before Galloway saw his chance. Suddenly he darted to one side and ducked around a tree, taking a quick turn of the rope around the bole. The move was so sudden that Curly, who only had dallied the rope around the saddle horn was caught unawares. Curly was no cowhand, although he had worked cattle to some extent, and he was careless by nature. Galloway's quick move in snubbing the rope around the tree not only brought his horse up short, but gave Galloway the instant he needed. Holding the snub tight with one hand he hastily kicked and shook the rope loose.

Curly wheeled his horse with a yell, but Galloway had ducked around a tree with others growing close beside it and it took Curly just a minute to find a hole through which he could guide his horse.

Curly grabbed for his pistol but a branch interfered. Galloway shook off the rope and ducking around the tree, jumped for Curly. Trying to pull back from the tangle in which he found himself, Curly felt a sudden heave on his stirrup as his leg was thrown up. He started to fall and tried to grab a secure hold on the pommel, but Galloway hacked at the fingers and Curly lost his grip.

He hit the ground with one foot caught in a stirrup and the frightened horse, backing and rearing, swung out of the trees and broke into a run.

Galloway staggered back, caught himself against a tree and slowly recovered himself. The horse went racing back toward the town, with Curly bouncing at every jump.

Glancing quickly around, he found Curly's pistol where it had fallen among the leaves. Hastily he checked the cylinder. Only three cartridges. Damn a man who didn't reload!

Holding the pistol in his hand Galloway started back for Shalako, only some two hundred yards away. He limped as he walked for his leg had been badly bruised when he had been dragged over the edge of the boardwalk.

He came into the head of the street and saw Curly's horse stopped in front of the saloon. Alf and the other Dunn were unfastening the rope. Berglund was kneeling beside Curly.

Galloway was within forty yards of them before Alf looked up. "I want my gun, Alf. Take it out mighty careful and put it down on the boardwalk."

Alf Dunn looked at Galloway. Hatred burned within him. At his feet lay Curly, dragged, torn and battered, injured badly, possibly dying. Always before the Dunns had had it their own way, and his hatred was filled with frustration and disbelief. This had never happened to the Dunns, it could not be happening.

Success corrodes, and the Dunns—always brutal, always cruel, always fighting a hit-and-run battle—had enjoyed success. Before their enemies could gird against them they were gone, miles away and with no idea of returning. In those swift strikes at unprepared ranches or communities they had been swaggering, triumphant and confident. Then Curly had been whipped by Flagan Sackett, a man who had just gone through a punishing ordeal, Jobe had been wounded, and the old Bull himself ignored. Now Curly had been terribly hurt in their moment of triumph, and here came the man who had done it, ordering him to throw down his pistol.

It was more than he could take. Alf said, "Pete, let's take him." Berglund left the ground in a long dive that carried him across the body of Curly and into the sparse grass beyond.

Alf and Pete with one accord had gone for their guns. Galloway's gun came up and fired. Alf turned halfway around and Galloway fired a second time. Alf Dunn backed up and sat down and Galloway's gun covered Pete even as Pete's gun came up. "Don't do it," Galloway said. "I'll kill you."

"And if he don't," a new voice said, "I will!"

Berglund, sitting up now that he was out of gun range, looked at the shaggy-haired big man in the faded red shirt and the black vest. A sheepskin coat was tied back of the saddle and there was a Winchester in the boot. The big man looked unkempt and almost unreal, for there was about him a wild savagery that was somehow shocking.

Galloway backed off a few steps to where he could see the newcomer. "Howdy, Logan! Nice to see you!"

He swung his eyes back to Pete. "You'd better take Curly home," he said, "and you tell Bull Dunn we want no more trouble. You brought it to us and by now you ought to have your belly full."

Pete snorted. "You think the old Bull will take this? He'll come in here a-foggin' it, mind you."

"His funeral. You tell him what I said. 'There's no need for all this shootin' and shoutin'.'"

Berglund got up slowly from the ground. "You two come in and I'll buy you a drink." He glanced at Logan. "I take it you're a Sackett?"

"Logan Sackett, from Clinch Mountain." He jerked his thumb toward Galloway. "He's a Cumberland Sackett. They're good people, too."

At the bar Berglund poured the drinks. "I think you boys are going to straighten out that Dunn outfit. They were riding roughshod over everybody."

"We want to ranch," Galloway said. "All we want is to make a home. If we get settled in, Tyrel and Orrin are coming up here. We'll have the whole family together."

Bull Dunn sat at the table in the long house and poured his tin cup half-full of whiskey, then replaced the jug on the table. "Stir up that fire," he said, speaking to no one in particular. "I want my coffee *hot!*"

An hour before, Pete Dunn had come in with the battered, half-alive body of Curly Dunn, and the body of Alf in which no life remained. And then, just a few minutes ago, Rocker had ridden in, leading the crew Bull had sent down to scatter the Sacketts' cattle.

Bull didn't need anyone to tell him they had failed. His eyes swept over the group of men wordlessly leading their horses into the corral.

"Where's Abel?" he asked, as Rocker swung off his horse in front of him.

"Dead. I wasn't there when it happened."

Bull turned on his heel and walked into the house. Now he was sitting at the head of the table, looking at what was left of his family and the few others he could trust.

The old Bull was shaken. For the first time in years things were going against him, and he was sure he knew why . . . because he had elected to stop.

Why stop? Was he getting tired? He tasted the raw whiskey, then turned the glass in his fingers.

That Curly . . . he couldn't do anything right. He goes into the woods with a tied-up man and comes out with his horse draggin' him.

"Vern," he glanced down the table at the sallow-faced young man, "you got it to do. Cut 'em down, one after the other."

Vern Huddy batted his eyes and looked sour, but offered no immediate comment. He had been studying out the country and he knew what he could do.

"That big man," he suggested, "the one Pete told of. That'll be Logan Sackett. He's an outlaw gunfighter. You all lay off him. He's a tiger."

"Let's have it," Bull said suddenly, "how did they get through with those cattle? I want to know."

"They had more men than we expected," Rocker spoke quietly. He was a young man of medium height, medium build, who carried himself with pride. "One of them, at least, was an Indian."

"There were several Indians," Ollie Hammer said. "They seemed to come right out of the ground and they kept those cattle running straight right down to the river. We never had a chance to scatter them."

"What happened to Abel?"

"He tried to draw against a Sackett. It was Flagan, the one who whupped Curly. Tin-Cup and me was with Rocker going after the cattle. There was no one else there who could take on Sackett."

Rocker had been toying with his cup. Now he lifted his eyes to his father. "Pa, we lost Abel. Curly is done up. If he lives he won't be any use to us until this here fight is all over. Jobe has got him a crippled arm. Alf is dead . . . I figure we'd better rattle our hocks out of here."

For a moment there was dead silence. Several stole looks at Bull, all were shocked. It was the first time any of them had dared suggest such a thing, and Rocker was the only one who could say it without a blow.

"You're talkin' crazy. When did we ever run from a fight?"

"Never. But nobody but a fool bucks a stacked deck. Pa, you don't know these Sacketts. There's a good many of them around the country, and when one of them is in trouble, they'll all come. We haven't seen anything yet."

"Vern will whittle 'em down."

"Maybe."

Vern's eyes came up sharply at the implied doubt. He started to speak, then held his silence.

"The Sacketts aren't nesters," Rocker continued. "They aren't just cow ranchers. Every one of them is a woodsman. They grew up feuding and fighting and they know all the tricks. I've heard about them for years. Tyrel and Tell are probably the best hands with guns, although Logan may be as fast.

"Flagan, Galloway, and Orlando are all good. I don't know about Parm Sackett, the one who bought those cattle they are bringing in."

"Rocker," Bull said impatiently, "that's fool talk."

"Maybe. But why buck a stacked deck? I think our luck's run out."

Bull glared at Rocker, but he made no reply. He gulped whiskey, took the coffee chaser, and waited. Something would come to him. It always had.

This country was too good to leave. He had hated the flat plains of Kansas, although he knew it was great cattle and wheat country. He liked eastern Colorado and Texas no better. He had wanted to stop nowhere until he rode into the valley of the La Plata.

It had looked easy. The country was wide open to settlement. The town of Shalako was small enough to be comfortable, and there weren't too many people around. They could move in, take what they wanted, and settle down to raise cattle and families. Controlling the largest number of voters he would be able to elect his own sheriff or marshal.

In just a few years they'd have some herds built up, stealing them down in New Mexico or Arizona if necessary, and they could hold this valley like a private place.

Then the Sacketts came in. They were warned, only they did not go. Curly had gone and picked himself a fight and gotten whipped, and that had been a blow. Bull Dunn knew how important is the reputation for invincibility, and the defeat of Curly by a man in bad physical condition threw a shadow over that reputation.

Suddenly everything had gone wrong.

Worst of all, Rocker was failing him, and Rocker had always been the smartest in the lot, the smartest and the quietest. The rest of them, well they were a wild lot, obeying nobody but him, listening to nobody but him. And until now they had believed nothing could whip them. Bull Dunn was not that kind of a fool. It was good for them to believe that as long as he, who was the boss, knew better. Bull Dunn had seen quiet communities suddenly rise up in anger, and suddenly the trees began blossoming with hanged men.

He knew all about that. He had left Virginia City, up in Montana Territory, just before the hanging started.

Just a hunch that he had, a sudden waking up in the morning with an urge to ride . . . and he had ridden.

When the news reached him that Henry Plummer and the rest of them were left dancing at the end of a rope he had known he was right.

Had his senses dulled over the years?

Was that what Rocker was feeling now? The Rocker had always been cautious, however. He was good with the six-shooter, probably the best Bull ever had seen, but he had a tendency to caution the others scoffed at, but not in front of the Rocker.

"All right, Rocker, you've been right before. We'll make one more try . . . just one. If that doesn't work we'll ride north out of here, head for Brown's Hole."

Rocker Dunn was uneasy, but he knew there was no use arguing, as even this concession was more than he had hoped for. And of course, the old Bull might know what he was talking about.

Yet he could not but remember the broken, bleeding body of Curly . . . he had never liked Curly, brother or no. There was something unhealthy about him.

Nonetheless, to see him come in like that . . . what was it about those Sacketts?

There was that Texas Ranger, McDonald, who said, "There's no stopping a man who knows he's in the right and keeps a-coming."

Maybe that was it.

Chapter XV

The cattle came in before noon of the day following the fight in the streets of Shalako. They came in bunched nicely and moving well. Parmalee had brought them over the trail losing no flesh and ready for a final polish before cold weather set in.

Yet the work had just begun with the bringing of the cattle, and while the Indians rode herd, I taken Galloway, Nick, and Charlie Farnum out to make hay.

There were high meadows where the hay was good, and we bought extra scythes at the store in town and went to work. Galloway and me, we'd had a spell of this as boys, and we went down the line cutting a wide swath, swinging the blades to a fine rhythm. Nick and Charlie were new at it and made more work of it.

We kept our guns handy, and usually one or two of the Indians were on lookout. We used the boys for this. They were sharp-eyed and eager to be helping, and lookout was warriors' work, so they loved it.

We saw nothing of the Dunns.

My thoughts kept a-turning toward Cherry Creek and the Rossiter place but there was just too much work for any one of us to shake loose. Anybody who thinks that ranching is just sitting and watching cows grow fat has got another guess a-coming. Ranching is mostly hard work, can-see to can't-see, as we used to say. Daylight to dark, for pilgrims.

Parmalee came out with a scythe on the third morning and threw us all a surprise. He was maybe the best of the lot at mowing hay. When it came to that, a body could see why. Down there in the flatlands they had more hay to mow than we folks on the uplands. Why, where I came from even the cows had legs shorter on one side than the other from walking on the sidehills!

The peaches and apples we grew on those mountains were so accustomed to the downhill pull you could only make half a pie with them because they insisted on slipping over to one side.

Bats and birds taken from those mountains down to the flatlands used to have to set down in the grass, they'd get so disoriented. They were used to flying alongside the land instead of over it.

If a man took a wrong step when plowing he was apt to fall into his neighbor's pasture or maybe his watermelon patch, which led to misunderstandings.

Church was down in the valley, so we never walked to church in the morning, we slid. We had the name of being good Christian folk in our part of the Cumberland because we just couldn't be backsliders.

Even Logan came out from town and took a hand at the haying. He was a powerful big man and he cut a wider swath than any of us. He'd put in a full day's work by morning and then he'd set by the fire and make comments about us being so slow. But we got the hay down and we got it stacked, and Logan proved a hand at that, too, but nobody could top off a stack as well as Parmalee.

Parmalee was a great one for reading, too, and he went nowhere without his books. I never could see why he needed them for he could remember nigh all he read, and it was a-plenty. Of a night by the fireside when somebody would start to tellin' stories of ha'nts and such, he would recite poetry to us. He'd set there

like he was telling a story and it would just come a-
rolling out.

He'd read poetry by Greeks even, and some by the
Frenchies, and he had a way of saying it that was a
caution. He and Nick Shadow would sit there spoutin'
poetry at each other, sometimes for hours. Whenever
one of them didn't start it, Logan would. Where he
picked up book knowledge I don't know, and he always
pleaded that he knew nothing, but he did know a sur-
prising lot. One time he admitted that he was snowed
in one winter with five books of which he read them
all, over and over. One of them was the Bible. He
knew all the stories but didn't seem to have picked up
much of the morals.

Logan Sackett was from Clinch Mountain, and those
Clinch Mountain Sacketts were rough, lawless boys.
They were fierce feuders and fighters and they went
their own way, most of them lone-wolfing it until trouble showed to another Sackett.

He was a story-teller when it came to that, and
could yarn on for hours about country he'd seen or
about bad men. Mostly in those days our world was
small. Folks got around a good bit and so we exchanged
information backwards and forwards of the country.
We knew about trails, marshals, bad men, bad horses,
tough bartenders and the like in countries we'd never
seen because word was sort of passed around.

Guns, riding, and cattle were our business, so we
heard plenty of stories about tough old mossy-horn
steers, about bad horses and men who could top them
off. Every outfit had at least one man who was salty
with a gun, and each one had a bronc rider. We
bragged on our roping or cutting horses, not often the
same ones, and how tough were the drives we made.
We ate beans, beef, and sourdough bread, and we had
molasses for sweetening. We slept out in the open, rain
or shine, and we rode half-broke horses that could
shake the kinks out of a snake.

It was a rough, hard, wonderful life and it took men

with the bark on to live it. We didn't ask anything of anybody and as long as a man did his work nobody cared what else he was or did.

Logan Sackett wasn't a bad man in the eastern sense. Out west he was. In the west a bad man was not necessarily an evil man or an outlaw . . . he was a bad man to tangle with. He was a man to leave alone, and such a one was Logan. He was mighty abrupt with a six-shooter, and if you spoke rough to him you had better start reaching when you started speaking, and even then you'd be too slow with it.

Logan had the name of being an outlaw. I suspect he'd rustled a few head of steers in his time, and maybe his stock didn't always wear the brands they'd started out with. I wouldn't be surprised if here and there he hadn't stood some stagecoach up while he shook the passengers down. About that side of his life I asked no questions. However, I'll bank on one thing. He never done anything mean or small in his life.

We'd all heard about Vern Huddy, but like everybody after awhile, you get careless. We'd been keeping an eye on the hills and the Indians were looking around for us, but all of a sudden one day there was a rifle shot and one of our Indians was down in the dirt and dead.

He was standing not three feet from me at the time and I had just moved over to dip up some beans from the pot and he had stepped up where I had been and was waiting with his plate. I was sure that shot had been meant for me, and Vern Huddy had sighted in, then maybe had taken his eyes away when he cocked his rifle and had squeezed off his shot before he realized there'd been a change. At least, that was how I figured it. I was sorry for that Indian, but glad for me.

We moved our camp deeper into the brush and all of us stayed clear of clearings.

"Somebody's got to go up there after him," Logan said.

"I'll go. I'm the best Indian. Every man has a pattern, I don't care who he is. Rifle shots are among the worst for that sort of thing. He's developed himself a style. If I study the places where he has been I can find the sort of places he likes to shoot from."

It made a kind of sense, so from that day on, I took to the hills.

Stalking a killer is no job for the weak-nerved. Sooner or later your killer is going to know he is being hunted and then he becomes the hunter.

If I found him soon I'd be lucky or unlucky, depending on who saw who first. The chances are it would only be after a painstaking search. So I taken a sight on the hills after dark. I set up a forked stick out there and a prop for the butt of my rifle and I figured the height of that Indian who was shot and where the bullet hit, then I sighted right back along my own rifle and pinpointed the area from which that bullet must have come.

Now I was sure Vern Huddy wouldn't be in that spot. He'd have moved, found himself a new location. Maybe he did not know he hadn't killed me, and maybe he did. By day I borrowed Logan's spyglass and studied the mountainside where the bullet had come from.

Only one thing I did do before I took to the woods. I went to Shalako to pick up a few things and ran smack-dab into Meg Rossiter.

She had come to town with her pa for supplies and the like. Town was town, even when it was so small, and a girl like Meg simply had to come in.

She had come up the steps to the store just as I rode up, and we stopped there for just a minute, she holding her skirt up just a trifle to clear it from the dust, and me just about to get off my horse. Finally I said, "Howdy, ma'am!"

"How do you do?" she said cool as you please. And when I swung down and stepped up on the porch she said, "I suppose that brother of yours is proud of himself."

"Galloway? What for?"

"For nearly killing poor Curly Dunn. That was just awful! He should be ashamed!"

Astonished, I said, "Ma'am, you don't have the right of it. Curly got the rope around Galloway unexpected, and was taking him into the woods. Curly was talking torture and the like. Galloway got free of him and Curly's horse dragged him, that's all."

"Galloway got free of him! That's likely, isn't it? Who helped him?"

"He was alone, ma'am. The rest of us was miles away with the herd."

Her eyes were scornful. "That's your brother's story. I don't believe any of it. Curly was not that kind of boy."

"I'm sorry, ma'am, but that's just the way it happened." Getting kind of irritated, I said, "Curly ain't much. He hasn't the nerve that Alf had or any of them, and he wouldn't be a patch on his old man. He's just kind of pretty and he has a real mean streak in him."

She just glared at me and turned away and flounced into the store. Well, I just stood there mentally cussing myself and all the luck. Here I'd been setting myself up, shaping up all kinds of meetings with her in my mind, but none of them like that. I never figured that Galloway's fracas with Curly would bother her none, least ways where I was concerned.

I guessed she was just fixed on Curly. She'd set her cap for him and she wasn't giving any thought to anybody but him.

Well, she could have him. I told myself that and stood there on the porch, wanting to go in the store and afraid she'd think I was following her, and wanting to follow her all at the same time. But I had to go in. That was what I'd come to town for.

Finally, I gave my hat brim a tug and ducked my head and went on in. Johnny Kyme, the storekeeper came over to me and said, "What can I do you for, Sackett?"

"About thirty feet of rawhide string," I said, "and a couple of those thin-bladed hunting knives." I also bought an extra hatchet and a few nails, with a few other odds and ends. I also bought me a pair of homespun pants (the brush doesn't make any sound when it rubs on them like it does on jeans, or even like on buckskin) I also bought a woolen cap with earflaps, although I wouldn't be using them. Where I was going a hat would be falling off, and I needed the bill of the cap to shade my eyes for good seeing.

Meg was coming right past me although she could just as well have gone the other way. She had her chin up and she was flouncing along, and suddenly I taken nerve and turned on her. "Ma'am, I'd admire to buy you a coffee over to the saloo——I mean, the restaurant, if you'll be so kind."

For a moment there she appeared about to turn me down, but I had something going for me that wasn't me. It was that she was in Town with a capital T, and a girl when she came to Town ought to see a boy. To sit and have coffee would be nice and she could think of herself as a great lady in Delmonico's or some such place.

She looked right at me, cool as you please. "Thank you, Mister Sackett. If you will give me your arm."

"I'll be back for all that," I said to Slim over my shoulder, and walked out of there, proud as could be, with that girl on my arm like we were going to a ball or something.

Now you have to understand about that saloon. It was a saloon, but one side of it was set up for an eating place where ladies could come if they wished, and when they were present the men kind of toned down the loud talk and the rough talk. Fact is, most of the men liked to see them there, added a touch of home or something, and most of us were a long way from womenfolks.

We went up those steps with me all red around

the gills from not being used to it, and trying not to look like this was the first time or almost.

Berglund, he came over with a napkin across his arm like he was one of them high-class waiters and he said, "What's your pleasure?" So we both ordered coffee, and he brought it to us, and then I'll be damned if he didn't fetch some cupcakes with chocolate high-grade all over the top. I never even knew he had such stuff.

When I said as much he replied, "Why, surely you understand that we only cater to the carriage trade? To the most elite clientele?"

I didn't know whether I was a elite clientele or not or if it was something I should shoot him for, so I tried to look stern and unconcerned all the same so he could either think I knew what he was talking about or irritated because he said it.

We sat there, sipping coffee and eating those cakes and talking. She started in about the weather just like we hadn't had those other words at all. I asked her about her Pa, and she asked me about Parmalee and Logan, and then somehow she got started telling me about a poem she'd been reading called the *Idylls of the King,* by somebody named Tennyson. I knew a puncher back in the Cherokee Nation by that name but it couldn't be the same one. The last time I saw him I don't think he could even read a book, let alone write one.

From all she had to say it was quite a book, and she was taken with this here Lancelot who went around sticking things with a spear.

There wasn't much I could say, not having read the book except to comment that it must take a mighty big horse to carry a man with all that iron on him. I don't think she thought that comment was very much in the line of her thinking. And she kept talking about chivalry and romance and her eyes got kind of starry until I began wondering where I could buy myself one of those suits.

Anyway, we had us a nice talk and I was right sorry to finish the coffee and those little cakes, but it did look like we were going to part friendly when all of a sudden she says, "You aren't the only pebble on the beach."

What she meant I didn't know for awhile, and then she said, "Mr. Huddy has been calling on me. He's very nice."

And before I thought what I was saying I said, "He's the one who has been trying to kill us. He hides up in the hills and shoots at us. He killed one of our Indian boys the other day."

Her face went kind of white and she jumped up so quick she almost upset the table, and then she said "Flagan Sackett, I never want to see you again!"

And she left out of there.

Berglund, he was polishing a glass and he said, looking at nobody, "It's better to have them mad at you than indifferent."

"Oh, shut up!" I said politely, and walked out of there, mad at me, mad at Berglund, and mad at Meg Rossiter.

Chapter XVI

What I said was true, but that didn't make any difference and it was the wrong thing to say right then, and to her. Meg Rossiter was a lone girl in a country filled with men, most of them older than her. There weren't any parties or dances or box-socials or the like to go to. She hadn't much chance to be a girl or to flirt.

Dumb as I was about women I'd watched them enough to know they like to play one man off against another, and like to feel wanted even if they ain't. Now Meg had set her cap or seemed to for Curly Dunn, and right away I come around saying he doesn't amount to much, and then Curly set to to prove me right.

No matter what she said to me she must have heard talk at the store. Johnny Kyme was a married man and his wife was a friend of Meg's and there was no nonsense about her. She knew what a skunk Curly was, but that didn't help Meg. Then we have a nice get-together like, and then she springs this Vern Huddy on me. Maybe she wants to make me jealous, maybe she just wants to feel courted, but right away I have to go make him out as bad as Curly or worse.

Back in the woods next morning we got together for a bit. Logan was there, Parmalee, Galloway, and Nick Shadow. Charlie Farnum came up as we started to talk. Everybody knew what I was starting out to do, and everybody knew it was a life-and-death matter. I

was going into the woods after a man who was a dead
shot, who moved like a cat, and had the senses of a
wild animal, or so we'd heard. One was going to be
dead before I came out of the woods. I knew it and
they knew it.

He seldom shot, almost never missed, and of the few
reported to have lived after he shot them, none could
say they had seen him or even knew he was about.

We talked a mite of everything else and then I got
up and taken my rifle. "I'm not going to take a horse,"
I said. "When you have a horse and you leave it
you've got to come back to it and the killer knows it.
I don't want to be tied to anything."

It was early morning and a mist lay in the valleys.
All was very still. At such times every sound in the
forest seems magnified if there is a sound, but I heard
nothing, moving carefully, taking my time. The route
I chose was roundabout. Where Vern Huddy would be I
had no idea, only that he would likely not be where I
would expect to find him.

My first destination was the spot from which he had
fired. I wanted to see what he liked in the way of firing
positions, and if possible pick up a clear track so I
could recognize it at any other time. So far I was working blind.

Taking my time, I worked my way through the
woods to the north, found the mouth of Little Deadwood Gulch and worked my way across it, checking for
tracks. I found the tracks of elk, deer, and some smaller
game, and started up the gulch, moving a few yards at
a time. Part ot that was the need to study the mountain to use the best cover, and part because of the altitude.

Just short of timberline, which I figured to be about
ten thousand feet up, I crossed the gulch and worked
my way along the flank of the mountain. By noon I
was holed up in a clump of spruce looking over at
Baldy.

For over an hour I sat there with Logan's spyglass,

which I'd borrowed, studying the side of Baldy from the bottom of Deadwood up to the top. First I swept it side by side at ten-foot levels, searching for life. Twice I glimpsed deer feeding quietly. Birds occasionally flew up, but none seemed disturbed.

Then I checked for possible approaches to Baldy, found a good one and promptly discarded it. Undoubtedly he had seen it, too, and would be watching it and occasionally making a sweep of the hillside. There was nothing.

Keeping low, I worked my way down into the gulch and up the other side. It needed an hour to find his firing position. He had built up a mound of earth on which to rest his rifle and he himself had a comfortable seat while he was waiting.

He had a good field of fire with no obstructions, and the actual distance was about four hundred yards, give or take a few. He had made no effort to conceal the fact that he had been here, probably doubting anybody would ever make a hunt for him or find the place. Or he might have left it for bait.

That idea hit me as I squatted on my heels and I just let myself go and hit the ground on my shoulder and rolled over into the brush just in time to hear the echo of a shot. It wasn't until I was thirty feet off and still moving that I remembered hearing that bullet. It had been a close thing.

He knew where I had disappeared and I had no idea where he was shooting from so I worked my way, moving swiftly but with no sound down the slope, then along the flank below his first firing position.

Was he pulling out? Or stalking me? No sooner had I asked the question than I knew the answer. He was stalking me. This Vern Huddy was confident. He might even be cocksure. He figured he was better at this game than anybody else, and maybe he was. If he was, I was a dead man.

Crouching for a moment in a sheltered place, yet one from which I could watch around me, I considered the situation. There was a good chance that after firing the shot that killed the Ute, he had pulled back to the slope above and just waited. He figured that somebody would come looking and he would get another one.

Some time passed and he had probably begun to relax. Maybe he was beginning to think nobody would come, and somehow I had slipped in and he hadn't seen me at first . . . which was almighty lucky for me. Or else there'd been a branch or something in the way of his shot and he had to wait until I moved.

There was nothing about this I liked. He was hunting me and that wasn't the way I wanted it. He'd probably had a few days to study that slope of Baldy and knew it better than me.

How about the back side? Maybe he knew nothing about that part of the mountain and mayhap I could just lead him around there and get him into country strange to both of us. To do that I had to stay alive long enough.

The worst of it was, he was above me. Like a ghost I moved along the mountainside, careful to break no stick, to let no stones rattle, to let no branch snap back. My clothes were soft, and the leaves brushing me made no sound that could be heard more than a foot away.

Did he have a horse hidden somewhere? Did he stay on the mountain at night?

One thing I had going for me. He had visited Meg Rossiter, and that could mean he moved on and off the mountain. There was every chance I could intercept him. Working my way on I went through a grove of aspen, circled some spruce, and then changed direction, going back and up on a diagonal line.

It almost worked. Suddenly, not a hundred yards off I saw a foot, gray moccasin, gray buckskin. My rifle came up and I fired . . . just as the foot was withdrawn. Instantly I put two shots into the brush above where I'd seen the foot, then slid thirty feet down the mountain, got up and ran through the brush. I ran swiftly and silently, swinging around to get above him.

There was no sound. My heart was pounding. Running at that altitude was not the thing to do, even though I'd spent a good time in the high-up mountains, nobody runs long up that high unless they've lived there for years.

There was small chance I'd hit anything. The shots into the brush were fired as much to make him wary as to hit. Of course, I wanted to nail him—I had to—but the chance of scoring was small.

When I'd gotten my breath back I listened, then went on up the slope, using all the cover I could find, until I was at least a thousand feet higher up the mountain. Then I studied the terrain all around me. Timberline was close above, which cut down my room to maneuver, but which also trimmed down his chance of getting around me.

My position was good. Only a thin line of wind-torn trees and rocks separated me from the barren top of the mountain. On my right the mountain was also bare for about four hundred yards, beyond that a clump of brush and trees, low growth, but enough to conceal. It was an island, however, and farther down, the slope was bare.

Before me was a weathered outcropping covered with lichen, the gnarled trunk of a weather-beaten spruce and low brush.

For a long time nothing moved below me, then suddenly a bird flew up. It might mean anything or nothing at all. I waited, rifle ready. Taking a piece of jerky from my small pack I began to chew on it while watching the slope.

Suddenly, I heard a rock strike, then a trickle of gravel. It was on the slope to my right, but nothing moved there. Flattening out, I studied the terrain to my left, and an instant later I caught the movement. He darted, just a shadow in the brush, running to get a little closer. I led him a little and fired. He hit the

ground and I fired again and again. Gravel rattled on
the slope below, but I did not move. If he was dead
it did not matter, if he was alive he would be waiting
for me to come to check on the results of my shots, and
I would do neither.

An hour passed . . . soon it would be sunset. Below
me I heard a muffled groan, but I remained where I
was. If he was dying, he could die without me. If it
was a trick, and I was sure it was, it would not draw
me out. Yet the coming sunset worried me for the sun
would be setting just beyond that patch of brush and
there would be a period when I could not see in that
direction due to the glare of the sun.

It was time to move. Swiftly and silently I went along
the mountainside in the opposite direction, avoided the
beginnings of Sawmill Canyon, crossed over it and
through a grove of aspen, some of the largest I had
ever seen. While I rested there I reloaded my rifle.

We could dodge around these mountains for weeks
taking potshots at each other, so something had to be
done to bring it to an end. I'd dusted him a few
times, I was sure of that, and I had done it to worry
him. I wanted to force him to great activity, for when a
man moves he takes a chance.

Night was coming on, so what would he do? If I
had a girl like Meg waiting I'd get shut of this black
old mountain and ride over there. He'd have to go
back across the La Plata to get over to Cherry Creek
and the Rossiter place, and there was a good chance
he'd left his horse over there, safely out of the way.

Well, I went down off that mountain fast. Circling
around, I got to our camp, got my horse and headed
for Cherry Creek. Getting my horse back into the brush
out of the way, I watched the ranch. Sure enough, it
wasn't more than an hour before that there Vern Huddy
came a-riding up like a Sunday cowboy all slicked out
in a fresh shirt and a black coat. He left his horse at
the rail and went up the steps.

I thought for a minute of finding myself a place out

there in the brush and pickin' him off when he came out. That's what he would have done to me. But dry-gulching just wasn't my way. I never could have faced up to Galloway and Parmalee if I'd got him that way . . . not to mention Meg if she ever found out. And she probably would . . . I'm not much good at keepin' quiet about something I'm ashamed of.

I got up and led my horse down, watered it, and led it to the hitch rail and tied it right alongside his. Then I went up the steps and rapped on the door.

Rossiter answered it. "Howdy there, boy! Good to see you! You're just in time for supper!"

He led the way into the dining room and you never saw such a picture. Vern Huddy's mouth must've have opened a good bit when he saw me. His face went kind of pale, he was that surprised. And Meg, she was surprised, too, but she wasn't surprised for more than a second and then she was pleased. Here she had two men a-courting her at the same time. Of course, she knew nothing about what had gone on up on the mountain that day.

"Mr. Sackett," she said primly, "I want you to meet Mr. Huddy."

Me, I grinned at him. "I've been looking forward to meeting Mr. Huddy," I said. "In fact, I've been thinking about him all day."

"You have?" Meg was puzzled.

"Oh, yes! He's the kind of man to keep you thinking about him. I can understand why a girl might give a good deal of thought to him, but ma'am, if you'll accept my word for it, he's a mite hard to pin down."

"Mr. Huddy and I," she said primly, "only met a few days ago."

"You'd better tie to him whilst you can," I said. "He may not be with us long." I was feeling good. I'd surprised them both and thrown them off balance and I was feeling in the mood for fun. Anyway, this was a chance to size him up a little. I'd never actually seen him before.

He was well set-up but a mite on the thin side, with a narrow, strict-looking face and not much sense of humor to him. It made him look a little older than I knew he was. He was mad now . . . I could see that plain as anything. I could also see that he thought well of himself and liked folks to fear him. Kill me he might, before this was over, but make me fear him he couldn't. He was just another man with a gun, and I'd seen a-plenty of them.

When he turned his head I saw a burned place on his forehead . . . it could have been from a branch but was more likely from a bullet. Had I been wrong about that groan I heard? Had he been knocked out and lying there all the time?

"Mr. Huddle," I said, "looks to me like you ran into something in the dark. Best be careful."

"My name is Huddy," he said testily, "and I shall be more careful. But I don't think the job I am doing will take me long. It is almost too easy."

"Now that's the way a man should look at his work," I said heartily. "I like to see a young man with ambition. That's what it takes to get ahead." Meg went for another platter of meat and I added, cheerfully, "Full of lead."

His eyes were ugly. He didn't find me much fun, I'm afraid. "You're easy," he said, "there's nothing to you, tomorrow—"

"Why not tonight?" I suggested. "We can ride down the road together, take our distance and shoot it out. You can have it as you like."

"I'm not a fool!" he said angrily.

Meg walked in then and smiled at us both. She was enjoying herself, and if she sensed anything in the air it surely didn't show.

"It's a real pleasure," I said, "meeting Mr. Huddle. I don't know many people in the San Juan Basin yet, and I'm most anxious to get acquainted." I looked over at him and smiled. "I understand you're connected with the Dunn family. Good neighbors," I continued.

"Why the other night when we were driving our cattle in, the whole lot of them waited for hours in the dark so they could be there to help us drive them in. And we've scarcely met. I call that neighborly," I said to Meg, "don't you?"

"I hadn't heard about it"—She was wary of me now. Something was going on and I knew she was remembering what I had said about Vern Huddy. He was no good at hiding his feelings either. A blind man could track the anger across his face—"but I would say that was very nice of them."

"I thought so. Especially as we didn't even know them, you know. All twenty or more of them waiting there in the dark, anxious to surprise us with their help. Fortunately we already had recruited some Indians to help us, so we had to express our appreciation an' run along about our business."

Rossiter was sitting there, saying nothing, missing nothing.

He was no fool and he had heard some of the talk that was going around. Also, the facts were obvious. We Sacketts had brought cattle into the country, a big herd and good stock, and we had shown every evidence of settling down.

The Dunns had built cabins but nothing else, making no effort to improve their land.

"We're going to build," I said to Meg, "and when we have the barn-raisin' we'll have all the folks over. We Sacketts sing . . . not me, I'm not much good at that, except for myself when I'm riding an easygoing horse . . . but the rest of them. We were Welsh and Irish away back, and we brought the singing notion with us.

"We'll have a barn-raisin', a house-warmin' and a sing. We've got some fiddlers amongst us, and we like a good time. Now I'm the serious one, me and Cousin Tyrel, I reckon, but Galloway, he's right amusing, downright amusing."

"I'd love a party!" Meg said. "Nobody's had one

since we've been here. There are scarcely enough people, I think."

"Ma'am, a western party never lacks for folks. I've seen cowboys ride from sixty, seventy miles away just to look at a pretty girl, let alone dance with her, and ma'am, you sure are the prettiest!"

Now like I've said, I ain't much on saying things to girls. I get tongue-tied and all, but being here with Vern Huddy across the table, and sort of ridin' him a mite, I just got shook loose and took to talkin' like Galloway or somebody. Maybe it was the excitement. I don't know much about causes and things, but I did not like Mr. Huddy. I've used a gun, but never to hunt a man down and kill him in cold blood. It's been in defense of life or property and when I'm forced to it. And I had doubts that Mr. Vern Huddy could meet anybody face to face.

Meg looked surprised and pleased, but she was also looking as if she couldn't believe it was me that said it. Neither could I.

"Nice to have new folks in the Basin, Mr. Huddle," I said. "We need folks who can help to build, to make this a better place to live. I look forward to the time when we'll have schools, churches and homes around about here. I suppose you're a prospector?"

"No, I am not." Vern Huddy looked up, his eyes on mine. "I am going into the cattle business."

"He's joking," I said, cheerfully. "At least I took him for a prospector. He was all over Baldy today, knocking on rocks, beating through the brush . . . he was surely looking for something and I am equally sure it wasn't cattle."

He ate with small appetite, while I felt good. Meg could really cook, and she was a right fine girl when it came to that, and I did justice to her food.

When the meal was over, Huddy got up. "I am sorry, but I must go." He was a little stiff and very angry.

"I reckon I'd better go too, then." I glanced at Meg. "You know, ma'am, there's been some shooting from the dark around here, and I think we'd be better off if we rode two together. Nobody's so apt to start shooting if there's two men."

"Oh!" she was disappointed. "Do you have to go?"

"Mister Huddy can stay if he wishes," I said blandly. "I have to be a-gettin' off down the road."

He had no idea of staying after I did and giving me the chance to lay for him beside the road, or to follow him to wherever he was going. So we walked out together.

Rossiter and Meg came with us. He gripped my hand. "It's been good to see you, Sackett," he said. "Come back any time."

He glanced over at Huddy. "Goodnight, Mr. Huddle," he said, and I chuckled. Then he and Meg went inside.

Vern Huddy wheeled his horse around and dropped his hand to his gun. Mine was covering him.

"Temper, Mr. Huddle," I said, "and there's a matter of common politeness. Never shoot anybody in somebody's yard who has been entertaining you."

My draw had been so much faster than his that he never cleared leather, and I know he thought I was going to kill him as he certainly would have killed me. "Now you ride out ahead of me, and don't try anything fancy."

He rode quietly until we neared the first bend in the road, then suddenly he was around it and running, and I let him go.

We knew what was coming, both of us, and the showdown would be tomorrow, in the mountains.

To follow down that trail now with him maybe laying for me would be crazy, so I turned off. There was a dim trail that led into the high-up hills just a mite west of Starvation Creek, so I taken it.

It wasn't until I was well up in the breaks before I realized that the head of Starvation Creek was where Nick Shadow's gold and diamonds were supposed to be hidden.

Chapter XVII

When Logan Sackett rode back to Shalako after the haying, Berglund's saloon was sporting a new sign—*The Gold Miner's Daughter*—and a painting of a well-endowed young lady in a flaming red dress and rings in her ears.

Berglund was standing outside looking at it. "Now there," he said, "is a work of art!"

"Who's the painter?"

"Who, he says. I am. Pat Berglund."

Logan studied it. "You better go back for more lessons," he said, "and I don't mean in painting."

They went inside and Berglund set out a bottle of beer. Despite the fact that the year was growing late, the day was hot. The beer was cold.

"How'd a Swede ever get the name of Pat?" Logan asked.

"My mother was Irish. I'm named for her brother who was a policeman in Boston."

He glanced at Sackett. "What are you named after? A berry?"

"A preacher . . . a circuit-ridin' preacher. He gave me a prayer book at my christening."

"You ever read it?"

144

"Sure. I know all the prayers. Trouble is, I never used 'em enough. I can quote the Bible by the chapter. My ma was a great one for camp meetings."

"You come to town alone?"

"Why not? I don't need any help."

"You may. Here come the Dunns."

Logan Sackett glanced out of the window, then finished pouring his beer. "There's only five or six of them. No use spoiling the fun by having Galloway along."

"You're not entirely alone," Berglund said. "I just saw Nick Shadow step into the store."

Bull Dunn got down off his horse. Ollie Hammer looked slowly around, then got off his horse.

Logan took a swallow of the beer. "Berglund, if there's anything in this place you don't want busted you better duck it out of sight. I have an idea those Dunns are hot for trouble."

The first one through the door was Tin-Cup Hone. He saw Logan Sackett and stopped dead.

"Howdy, Tin! You're a long way from home, and you've got a horse."

"What's that mean?" Hone said warily.

"A man with a horse who's so far from home ought to be riding it," Logan said cheerfully.

"I'll stay."

"All right. When I go to funerals I always admire to see a handsome corpse. They'll fix you up real pretty, Tin."

Red had come in from the back door. "Take his advice, Hone. I got that advice one time and I pulled out. I ain't never been sorry."

"He's alone, ain't he?"

"No, Tin, he ain't. Nick Shadow's down the street, and Nick is just plain poison with a six-gun and he's one of the kind who just don't care. He's like the mule who butted his head into a tree, an' somebody asked if he couldn't go around it and they answered sure, but he just didn't give a damn. Shadow is like that. Did you ever buck a man who just plain don't care? Everybody dies but him. I seen it before."

Hone walked slowly to the bar. "There's six men out there and four more a-coming up. Not even Logan Sackett and Nick Shadow can buck them odds."

Red chuckled. "You ain't countin' me. I been on the wrong side too often. This time I'm on the right ride. I think I'm as good as you, Tin.

"And I'll tell you something else. Galloway was cuttin' a tree down in the breaks by the river and when he came out he saw you Dunns a-coming. Right now him and Parmalee and that breed of theirs, Charlie Farnum, they're right over yonder in the livery stable."

"Gimme a beer," Tin-Cup said. "It'll be thirsty, riding."

"Drink it on your horse," Logan said, "they're going to open the ball."

Bull Dunn came through the door. He saw the back door closing after Tin-Cup Hone and he turned his cruel eyes on Logan. "Heard about you," he said.

"I usually fight with a gun," Logan said, "but this time I'm going to whip you with my hands."

Dunn glanced at him, disgusted. "Don't be a fool. Nobody ever came close."

"Maybe they didn't do it right," Logan said, and hit him.

He had put the beer down on the bar and he simply backhanded Bull Dunn across the mouth, smashing his lips. Bull Dunn was huge and powerful, but Logan Sackett, while considerably lighter, was almost as tall and a man with huge shoulders and chest. His blow did not even stagger Dunn when it mashed his lips, but Logan let the impetus of the blow turn him, so he threw a left hand at Bull's head. The bigger man pulled his head aside and grabbed Logan with his huge arms.

Logan shoved the butt of his palm under Bull's chin, forcing his head back, then he struck him twice in the ribs and shoved him off. Dunn struck out hard and knocked Logan into the bar, then charged him, head down and swinging. Logan rolled free, smashed a wicked short right to the side of the face that split Bull's ear, showering him with blood.

Bull turned like a cat, landed left and right to the head and rammed in again, but Logan slapped a hand down on Dunn's head, thrusting it down to meet Logan's rising knee. Dunn staggered back, his nose and mouth a gory wreck.

Then toe-to-toe they began to slug, smashing punch after punch, neither man trying to evade, each one soaking up punishment. Logan was a little the faster, Dunn the heavier and perhaps the stronger. It was rough, brutal, and beautiful to watch. People crowded into the room. Up and down they went. Logan pulled free and knocked Bull Dunn down with a smashing right, but the big man lunged up from the floor, grappled Logan about the hips and lifted his body clear of the floor, then slammed him down across a table, which crashed beneath them. Bull dove at him, but Logan hit him with a short right to the face, then heaved him off. Both men came up together. Dunn swung a kick for Logan's groin, and Logan brought his knee up across in front of him, blocking the kick.

Then he walked in, smashing blow after blow to Dunn's face. Bull broke away, charged again and threw Sackett hard. Dunn jumped for Logan's face with his boots and Logan rolled aside. He got to his feet in time to meet Dunn's rush. Again they stood slugging, grunting with every punch. Shirts torn and faces bloody, they swung and swung, but Logan was slowly pushed back by the larger man's brute strength. Back he went down the room, then suddenly he seemed to weaken, and fell back against the bar.

Seeing victory, Dunn set himself and drew back his fist for a finishing punch, and Logan Sackett, who had faked his weakness, threw a short inside right. It dropped like a hammer to Dunn's chin inside of his swing, and stopped the big man flatfooted. Stunned,

Bull Dunn stood, his fist poised, and then Logan Sackett punched short and hard with both fists—a left to the face, then a ripping right uppercut to the midsection.

Dunn's knees sagged and Logan Sackett whipped another right to the face.

Bull went down. He hit the floor on his knees and Pete Dunn screamed as if stabbed. "No! No, pa! They can't lick you! Nobody can!"

Bull Dunn lunged up, dazed and shaken, staring blindly for his enemy. Logan Sackett was pouring beer into a glass, and Dunn lunged at him. Logan Sackett lifted a foot to fend him off—boot against Dunn's chest, knee bent. Then he straightened the knee and Dunn staggered back and fell again.

Logan Sackett rinsed his cut mouth with a swallow of beer, then gulped it down. "Stay down, you damn' fool," he said. "You're game enough."

Bull Dunn stared up at him. "I wish . . . I wished I could get up, damn you, I'd—"

"Have a beer," Logan said. "You fight pretty good."

He walked over and taking the bigger man's arm, helped him to his feet where he half fell against the bar. Logan shoved a beer in front of him. "It's cold," he said. "Tastes good after a fight, and before a long ride."

Bull looked at him. "You don't need to grind it in," he said. "I should have listened to Rocker."

It was hot in the street outside. Nick Shadow stood in front of the livery stable, well out of sight. Galloway was in the doorway, staying in the shade to see better. The sound of fighting from the saloon was finished.

"Somebody won," Shadow said, "and somebody lost."

Parmalee came from the store. "I guess it's all over," he said.

"Not quite," Ollie Hammer said, "not quite."

"Why not?" Parmalee suggested. "It's finished in

there. If your people won they'd be out here in the street, looking for the rest of us."

"What about your crowd? Won't they come out?"

Parmalee smiled. "They know we can handle it," he said calmly.

"You? You dude? You're leavin' it to Shadow, or that cousin of yours, or whatever he is."

"Second cousin, I believe. Oh, they could handle it all right, Hammer, but if you prefer me, I'm at your pleasure. Draw when you will."

"Now there's the gent," Ollie Hammer said, " 'draw when you will' " he mimicked. "All right I'll——"

His hand flashed for his gun.

Parmalee's gun was an instant faster, his shot smashed Ollie's gun hand and the gun fell into the dust. "And to show you that was intentional," Parmalee said, and he fired again, the bullet smashing the gun's butt as it lay in the dust. "I really don't want to run up a score, Hammer," Parmalee said. "I'm a ranching man, not a gunfighter."

"You ain't seen the last of this," Ollie Hammer said. "Huddy is still up on the mountain. When he's finished there won't be a Sackett left. And then there's Rocker."

Parmalee put his gun back in the holster and walked across to Galloway. "What about it? Shall we go up there and help Flagan?"

"Flagan don't need help. And right now he knows he's up there alone. He can shoot at anything that moves. If we go up it'll just complicate things. Leave him be."

He hitched up his pants. "Let's all go home. We got some siding to build. We're goin' to have a barn-raisin' soon, and we're going to build us a house.

Galloway gestured toward the hills. "I want to come out of a morning and look up at those hills and know nothing can be very wrong as long as there's something so beautiful.

"My pa used to say that when corruption is visited upon the cities of men, the mountains and the deserts await him. The cities are for money but the high-up hills are purely for the soul.

"I figure to live out my life right here where I can hear the water run and see the aspen leaves turn gold in the autumn and come green again with spring. I want to wake up in the morning and see my own cattle feeding on the meadow, and hear the horses stomping in their stalls. I never had much chance for book learnin', but this here is a kind of book anybody can read who'll stand still long enough. This here is the La Plata country, and I've come home."

Chapter XVIII

The wind sang a broken song among the sentinel trees. Below the scattered outposts were massed the dark battalions of the pines like an enemy ready to march against me, and somewhere along the lower edge of that black line lay the man who held the rifle that had shot me, and the bullet with which he intended to kill me.

Vern Huddy had the taste of blood upon his lips, and was a-thirst for more, and I lay with my body torn by his bullet, shuddering with every breath, my coat gone and night a-coming on, waiting for him to make his move.

Only thing good about it was that he didn't know exactly where I was. His bullet got me most of an hour before as I dove for shelter, but I'd wormed and scrambled and crawled some little distance since then.

I gouged snow from the almost frozen remains that had backed up against a rock near me. I let a handful melt in my mouth and felt the delicious coolness of it going down my throat, through my body.

Moving stones from under me I piled them around, digging myself deeper against the cold and Huddy's bullets. The weakening was upon me, and for two hours before the bullet hit I'd been driven and out-

151

flanked at every turn by a man who was a past master at his trade, and who knew now that I was somewhere along timberline with nowhere else to go. In his heart he was sure he was going to get me.

This was my last stop. Whatever happened must happen here. I told myself that and I believed it. I could not go back because it was a wide-open space and even in the night there would be enough light to see me against that gray-white expanse.

The hole made by the bullet I had plugged with moss, and now I was waiting for him to come in for the finish. If he came before I passed out I might get him, and if not he would surely get me.

It was growing dark. Down in the valleys below it was already dark and people were sitting down to their tables to eat warm suppers in pleasant surroundings. Meg Rossiter was down there preparing supper for her pa, or helping, and around the campfire my brother and the others would be wondering where I was.

Easing my long body to a better position, I waited. He did not know where I was and I did not know where he was, and each needed to know. Squirming deeper into the gravel, I shivered against the cold. It was growing late in the year and at this, nearly twelve thousand feet of altitude, it could become icy by night.

This was a different peak from the night before, unknown to both of us. They called it Parrott or Madden . . . the two were side by side and I was not sure which we were on. I didn't know the country that well.

Digging a fragment of jerky from my pack, I began chewing on it. That pack of mine was almost flat, just a place to carry a few pieces of bread and meat to sort of tide a man over.

I'd lost a good bit of blood and the shock of the bullet had been great. It seemed to have struck the top of my hip-bone, knocking me down and numbing my leg, but then it had glanced into the flesh and had gouged a deep hole.

Even if Huddy did not get me I'd be lucky to last

the night. The blood drained from me and the icy cold would take care of that. Suddenly something moved, and leaving my rifle alone I drew my pistol . . . how could he have come so close!

There was a low whine . . . *that damned wolf!*

How could he have followed me up here? But why not? He seemed to be haunting me. Now I've known wild animals to do some strange things. I heard of a panther one time who followed a boy two miles through a dark forest only a few feet behind him, the boy talking to it all the while thinking it was his dog. Then he called out to the house and when they opened the door they all saw the panther . . . it ducked off into the brush.

I taken a small bit of the jerky from my pack and said quietly, "Here, boy!" And tossed it out there.

Eager jaws took it, and I could hear the chewing. I began talking to it in low whispers, and calling it to me. After a long while it did come, crawling over the bank on its belly as if it knew enough to keep down, and then waiting while I talked to it. Suddenly it crawled closer.

Seen up close, even in the almost dark, it looked like a wolf and yet not quite like one. In fact, it might have been half dog.

My hand reached out to it. The wolf growled a little, but warningly rather than threateningly, then it sniffed of my fingers, seemed reassured and crept closer. I put a hand on it, then listened, but heard nothing. My hand brushed the thick ruff and started to scratch.

"My God!"

The expression was startled from me, for around the neck of the wolf was a collar, a collar so tight the poor animal was almost strangled!

"Why, you poor devil!" I reached for my knife and talking to it all the while, slipped the knife under the collar. The wolf began to gag and choke, but he seemed to know I was trying to help, and then that razor-sharp blade cut through the collar and it came loose.

The effort taken a good bit from me, but I lay there, whispering to that wolf that he'd be all right now. The poor thing had been follerin' me around for all this time, figuring I could help it. Must be that some man had at one time had it for a pet, had put the collar on when it was small, and the wolf had gone back to the woods or maybe the man had died. Then the wolf had grown and grown until the collar was choking it. No wonder it was so hungry for the small fragments I threw out. It could swallow them.

I kept my hand on the ruff and kept talking to it, and oddly enough, the wolf showed no idea of leaving. He crept closer, and even licked my hand. And the first thing I knew I'd fallen to sleep.

It must have been the warmth of the big animal lying close thataway, and part of it was that my attention had been torn from the main issue and I forgot about staying awake. Anyway, I slept.

And then I heard a low, ugly growling alongside of me and suddenly I was awake. Just the glimpse of the stars showed it was past midnight.

"Quiet, boy!" I whispered, putting a hand on the wolf, and it quieted down, but its ears were pricked and it was looking right straight ahead.

Me, I eased my pistol out and rolled away from the wolf so if I drew fire it would not get hit.

He was coming in. I heard a foot grate against gravel and then he was there, black against the sky.

The wolf suddenly sprang away and his gun came up and I said, "Don't shoot. It was just a wolf."

"A *what?*"

"A timber wolf," I said. "He's a friend of mine."

"You're crazy," he said. "Out of your head."

"You going to kill me now?" I asked, conversationally.

"And enjoy it," he said, "and then I'm going down to see Meg. Nobody will ever find you up here. I'll just leave you for that wolf or whatever it is."

My pistol was in my hand but he hadn't seen it.

He was standing about a dozen feet away and he had a rifle and he was holding it in one hand pointing it at me. It began to look like a Mexican stand-off, with both of us dying up here.

"Ever see a wolf come to a man before, Huddle?" I said. "If you'll stop and think, that there's impossible. Up in the mountains of Tennessee we know all about wolves and such, like ha'nts and werewolves."

He was suddenly still, like he almost stopped breathing. "That's fool talk," he said. "I'm going to kill you, Sackett."

"If you do," I said, "you'll never get off the mountain. That there's what the Indians call a medicine wolf. He'll get you sure. Tear you to bits . . . unless you got a silver bullet."

"You're lying!"

There was a low growl from the bushes to his right, and as he spun slightly toward the sound I lifted my gun and shot him.

His rifle went off and spat sand into my face. His movement must have deflected it just by a hair, just enough to save my bacon.

He was down, but I could see the glint of the rifle barrel as he moved it toward me. I shot him again.

The rifle fell from his hands as he rolled over on his side. I stood up. "No! No!" he whispered. "Oh, no, *no!*"

"You gave it to a good many, Huddy," I said. "You shot that poor Indian who worked for me, shot him when he didn't even know, and when no enemies were around. He never had a chance to lift a hand. Now you know how it feels."

"No . . . not me." He was whimpering like a child. "Not me!" And I had it in me to feel sorry for him. Somehow his kind never figure it will be them. They always kill; they are never killed. That's the way they see it.

Taking up his rifle I backed off a little, still wary

of him because he was packing a six-shooter, but I needn't have been because he was dead.

The wolf moved out there in the dark and I said to him, "Come on, boy, we're going home now."

Picking up his collar because I wished to see it by daylight, I started down the mountain in the first gray of dawn, and the wolf—or dog-wolf which he seemed to be—fell in behind me. Not too close, not too far.

Looked like he'd been lonesome for a man to belong to, and when he saw me and I tossed him that meat back yonder he figured I might be the one to help him out of the trap that was sure to kill him sooner or later.

We started down the mountain, but we stopped down there where Starvation Creek flows out of the rock, and I hunted around for that gold and found it. Taken me only a few minutes and I had to rest, anyway, with my wound and all.

I was in bad shape again, but this time I was going home and I had a friend with me. The gold was heavy so I only taken one sack of the stuff, just to throw on the table in front of Nick Shadow, and say "This what you were lookin' for?"

The sky was all red, great streaks of it, when I walked across the meadow toward the fire. Soon as I felt better, I was going over to see that Meg girl. She'd want to hear about my wolf.

The boys came out and stood there staring at me. "It's Flagan," Galloway said. "I knew he'd be coming in this morning."

"Boys," I said, "you got to meet my wolf. Take good care of him, I—"

Well, I just folded my cards together and fell, laid right down, dead beat and hurt. But it was worth it because when I opened my eyes, Meg was there.